CRUISE CONTROL

WATCHERS CREW BOOK 2

INES JOHNSON

THOSE JOHNSON GIRLS

ONE

I knew I should've blown my boyfriend this morning, but I had to get to my biology tutor. I'd gotten a series of B's in Biology 101 and it was messing with my 4.0 GPA. So this morning, while he was still sleeping, I decided to blow off giving my man some head and went off to tend to my education instead of tending to his dick.

It was the wrong decision.

There he was, standing in the corner of a bar with his crotch pushed into the hip of some vapid blonde. She giggled and flicked her hair over her bare shoulder as he whispered in her ear. The strobe lights on the dance floor made a sweep over them. The light shone directly into her eyes, and out her ears.

I tried to look away, but I couldn't. The skin around my eyes bunched up like the blinders they put on horses to keep out distractions and keep the animal's attention focused on the direction it needed to go. I stood there and watched Sergio's hand trace over the speed bumps of her breasts. Those hands, which had been in my pussy just last night, took the sharp curve of the blonde's waist and came to rest on the turnpike that was her ass.

The journey was no accident. When I confronted him this time, he couldn't tell me she bumped into his hand. He wouldn't convince me he was just helping her out by reaching for something in her pocket. These were horse blinders over my eyes, not sheep's wool.

I would not accept another lame ass excuse. I would not allow myself to look the other way and pretend I didn't see what was right in front of me. Not this time.

Fuck! Why the hell hadn't I skipped my tutoring session?

I heard my mother's voice in my ear. She always railed that the more educated the woman, the less likely she was to get a husband, especially if she has any color to her skin. The pickings were slim for smart women of color, my momma insisted. When I told her I'd have both, an education and a man, she raised an eyebrow at me and turned back to look out the living room window to perform her one and only task, which was waiting for my father to come home so she could take his shirt and clean off the lipstick stains that weren't her shade of red.

From my position at the bar, I saw the pink lipstick stains on Sergio's collar. I'd picked out that shirt for his birthday last month.

I wasn't even angry any more; I was just tired. Tired of fighting the reality that sooner or later all men cheat. It's just in their DNA. Thanks to my biology lesson, I learned that it's more than human males' DNA. The tendency is in all male animals. My tutor, Ellie, said it's in insects too. Few male species are faithful to their mates.

I knew this. I'd learned it at a young age. I'd had the message reinforced since I began dating in middle school. My cheating-boyfriend-radar had been fine tuned before my junior year of high school.

With Sergio, I'd figured out his phone passcode after our third date, and got access to all his texts, social media, and emails. I'd found him so easily tonight because I'd hacked the GPS in his car (and Momma said my education would get me nowhere with a man). I knew that he'd been cheating since last week. Now, it was just a question of did I want to put in the work to get him back into my bed tonight?

The forecast called for a storm later on tonight. Thunder always woke me up, and I hated waking up in bed by myself. My fingers hovered over the top button of my blouse; ready to release my girls to draw my man back to me. But just then Sergio looked up and caught sight of me. His expression halted my trigger finger. I watched, frozen, as Sergio fit three emotions into two seconds, much like our love life.

His first expression was of shock. His eyes widened as he looked up and recognized that it was me. Then his eyes dropped into guilt. That look sparked hope in my heart.

Maybe this could be salvaged. Maybe I wouldn't have to sleep alone tonight. That blonde was clearly hitting on him. He was just being nice.

He hadn't groped her ass. He'd been shoving the scrap of paper with her number on it back into the back pocket of her jeans. He had to push his fingers into her ass to get it all the way into her pocket because her jeans were so damn tight. It was loud in this place. That's why he leaned down to whisper in her ear; to communicate to her that he had a girlfriend.

But then Sergio's face morphed into a sneer. His head tilted to the side. His mouth opened as though he let out a single, huffing bark of laughter.

The music blared, but I heard that huff of laughter from across the room. More than waking up alone to the sound of thunder, I hated that look of pity my exes got on their faces when it finally clicked for them the depths I went to track them down and try to hold on to them.

I couldn't handle that look, not tonight. I turned my back on my ex and searched desperately for a Plan B. I zeroed in on the first thing I saw with pecs and biceps.

Dark eyes stared back at me through almond-shaped eyelids. Intelligence oozed out of the corners of those long lashes. Generally, I didn't prefer my victims to be smart. I liked them with big dicks and small brains. It made them easier to control when I could simply yank on the biggest parts of their body to get their attention. This guy's dark eyes were so clear I saw my reflection in the dim lighting. It looked as though he'd seen everything that had just gone down and knew what was about to happen next.

"Do you have a girlfriend?" I have no idea why I asked him that question. Maybe because I believed in karma and I didn't want it coming back around on me for what I was about to do.

"No." His voice was quiet, a whisper over his silky tongue, but I heard him clearly. He said that one word with a slight raise of his eyebrow, as though the concept was juvenile, ridiculous.

He was likely a player, had to be with those good looks and easy confidence. He was Asian, but I wasn't down enough with Asian culture to know which country.

His skin had a deep tan to it. His dark hair rested just above his eyebrows in a wave, as though he'd swept it out of his way just a moment ago. It fell back over his eyes as he tilted his head down to survey my body. I could tell that I met his approval when his nostrils flared as they swept over my breasts. He suited perfectly for my plan.

"Good," I said just before I reached up to pull his head down to my mouth.

He didn't jerk back from me in disgust. Neither did he gasp as though surprised by my actions. He didn't open his mouth and try to shove his tongue down my throat. Neither did he open for me as I licked sensually at his lips. He just stood there, letting me lick my tongue futilely. And then, I felt his hand move between us.

My tongue rested on the divot at the middle of his lower lip as my attention focused on the track of his hand. His fingers lightly traced down my side. It was a gentle touch. It skittered the fabric of my blouse, giving only a bit of pressure to the skin beneath. He continued the motion across my belly, and on down to my pubic bone. Before he got those sneaky fingers in between my legs, I gasped and pulled my mouth away from him.

"What do you think you're doing?" I shuffled back half a step, but then I stopped and pressed my thighs together. The areas where his fingers had contacted my skin through the fabric of my clothes all tingled.

"You tried to put your tongue in my mouth." He leaned back against the bar. "I tried to put my hand in your pussy."

I straightened my shoulders with a huff while my pussy buzzed at the sound of its name on this guy's tongue. "I was only kissing you."

"I don't see a difference," he shrugged.

From the corner of my eye, I saw Sergio, my boyfriend. Strike that- my ex boyfriend. Sergio, my ex boyfriend, was making his way over to us. He fumbled a step as he evidently caught sight of the man standing with me. Sergio's hand went to his chin. He scratched at the pity he'd been about to present to me. That pitiful expression was slowly crumbling away.

"Look," I turned back to the guy at the bar. "I just caught my boyfriend cheating on me."

"Boyfriend?" There went that eyebrow again.

I didn't like the way he said that word with a smirk. Instead of the twenty-year old modern woman I was, I felt he was looking at me as though I had on a poodle skirt and I'd just told him my steady guy offered me a promise ring.

The truth was Sergio had never promised me anything. I'd called him my boyfriend, but he'd never confirmed it by calling me his girlfriend in return. Nor had we exactly said we'd be exclusive to each other, but we had been screwing around for over a month now. Thirty plus days of fucking and blowjobs should imply exclusivity.

The Asian guy looked around the dance floor. "Your man is in here fucking another girl?" His voice was full of interest, as though he would like to see that show.

"No," I grimaced. "He was talking to some girl

over in the corner. He just saw me and he's headed this way."

Just like Sergio scratched his chin a second ago, this guy's hand rose and scratched as he considered my words. "He was just *talking* to some girl?"

It wasn't pity on his face, but I still felt like he was speaking to me as though I were a child coming to him with an adolescent's concern, like someone was playing with my Ken doll without my permission.

"Can you just pretend to be here with me?" I said. "Just for a minute, and then I'll leave you alone. Please?"

His calm face studied me. Then his dark eyes flicked over my shoulder. He reached up and wrapped an arm around my waist. "Sure, but only because I like how you beg."

"Kira?"

I stiffened at the sound of Sergio's voice behind me. In front of me, my eyes pleaded with my sexy decoy to be cool. In response, the corner of his sexy mouth ticked up. Decoy man moved his hand from my hip and rested it on my ass. I pursed my lips, but I let it stand and turned around.

Sergio stood there, alone. I saw the blonde standing in his wake. I placed my hand on the Asian guy's chest. I had to take a moment to enjoy the play of muscles there beneath his soft cotton shirt. I was a sucker for a well-defined chest.

I put on my brightest smile. "Hey Serg, I thought that was you over there. You having a good time?"

Sergio looked between me and the Asian guy, then over his shoulder at the blonde. "Yeah, I'm just hanging out with some friends." He turned back. "I thought we had plans tonight?"

I arranged my face into a theatrical wince. "I didn't think we'd set anything firm. I'm not sure when I'll be home."

My partner in this lie took the hint and pulled me closer to him, nuzzling my ear. "*If* you'll be home," the Asian said in my ear, but loud enough for Sergio to hear.

I giggled like one of those vapid girls that I couldn't stand. "Sorry, Serg. Maybe some other time?"

"Forget it, you cunt. I don't do sloppy seconds."

I saw red. Before I could launch into an attack, my decoy stepped up.

The Asian guy locked his arm around my waist, his fingers dug into my ass. "You're the sloppy one if your girl needs to go out and look for somebody else to satisfy her."

Sergio reared up. He thrust his chest out and bared his teeth. "She's not even worth it. She can't fuck for shit."

Again I was ready to stand up for myself and lay into Sergio, but the Asian guy's hand, which was still on my side, dug into me, commanding me to stay put and quiet.

He tucked me behind him and squared off, planting his feet wide. From over his shoulder I saw the smile on his face, challenging Sergio to make a move. Sergio was bigger than this guy. That didn't seem to bother my decoy. A crowd gathered. A bouncer came over.

Sergio took a step behind the bouncer. "Yeah, you better hold me back. You don't want to mess with me, man."

The bouncer escorted Sergio to the front door. He left me and the Asian guy alone without a second glance.

Once Sergio was out the door, the Asian guy offered me his hand. "Come on."

I put my hand in his and we headed towards the exit. In the dark night's sky, gray storm clouds overran the deep blue. The rumble of thunder could be heard in the distance. I wrapped my arms around myself in the humid air as I thought about the long, sleepless night ahead of me.

"Thank you," I said to my rescuer. "I appreciate your help with that."

He shrugged as though it meant nothing. It probably hadn't. He'd gotten to grope a woman and flex his muscles. Now, he'd go off and fuck one of the many women who had eyed him appreciatively on his way out the door.

"But you know," I said, "you didn't have to try to put your hand up my skirt."

"You tried to put your tongue in my mouth."

"I kissed you. You groped me."

"Yeah, I still don't see the difference," he said. "Do you know how many germs are carried in the human mouth? A woman's pussy is far more hygienic a place for a man to put his tongue than in their mouth. A man's dick is also a more hygienic thing to put into your mouth than someone else's tongue."

Was this guy for real? "So, what? I violated you?"

"Yes. If you'd asked me to kiss you, I would've said no. I don't know you or where your mouth has been. If you'd asked me to eat out your pussy, I would've said yes. Would you like me to eat out your pussy?"

I stumbled down the last step. "No."

"Are you sure? You look like you need a good release after fucking that prick. When's the last time you came?"

"None of your business."

"Would you like to make it my business?"

I couldn't respond. My body was tingling again at all the places where he'd touched me; the left side of my body where his fingers had traced. My hip, my ass, my stomach, and just below my pubic bone.

Sergio was full of shit. I wasn't a bad lay. He never complained before. I always got him off. But it was never the other way around. This guy beside me gave me the feels with my clothes on.

"I'd like to make it my business," said the man who'd made me tingle with a touch. "You put your tongue in my mouth. Let me put mine in your pussy, and then we'll call it even."

From the corner of my eye I saw Sergio putting the blonde into his car. The best way to get over one guy was to get under another. That's how I got over the guy I dated before going out with Sergio. Why mess with tradition?

Plus, this guy was cute. Those dark, intelligent eyes of his were glazing over in desire for me. I'd got an impression of his size when I'd pressed myself up against him. That thing had to be bigger than his brain. I wouldn't mind leading it around for a bit.

Why not? I sure as hell didn't want to go home alone after that scene. And who knows? He might make an excellent new boyfriend.

"What's your name?" I said.

"You can call me Owl."

"Hi, Owl, I'm Kira."

TWO

Owl led me around back to the parking lot. On the way there he tucked my hand into the crook of his arm, just like they did on those old Masterpiece Theater period movies.

"We're going to fuck, not court." I pulled my arm away. That public display of affection was more than I'd ever received from any other boyfriend.

Owl's chuckle was light as it breezed across the tip of my ear. "Should I push you into the alley, shove up your skirt, and fuck you in front of all these people?" He stopped walking, turned, and faced me. "Would you like that, Kira?"

There were people on the streets, but none in the actual parking lot. I wasn't into public sex, but the way he looked at me, the way he'd said that, my brain -no, my pussy- actually considered it. Too bad he was kidding.

He was kidding, right? We faced off in the middle of the lot. He stared at me, waiting for my answer. My mouth wouldn't work.

But then he grinned. "My car's just over here."

Owl put my arm back into the crook of his elbow and led me over to a red Honda Civic with a black and gold dragon painted on the side. The car was sandwiched in between three other cars that looked like they belonged in the movie *The Fast and the Furious*. There was a black Charger, a green Audi R8, and a gray BMW coupe.

How did I know the make and models? I'd had a lot of boyfriends. All the cars had unique paint jobs, but I didn't get a chance to admire them in the dim street lighting. Owl opened the rear passenger door of the Civic for me.

I turned to him and frowned. "Aren't you taking me home?"

He leaned into me, pressing my body into the frame of the car. "You shouldn't go home with strange men, Kira. You don't know what they might do to you."

It was smart advice that I'd ignored for a good portion of my adult life. I'd gone home with a ton of strange men. The worst thing to happen to me so far was waking up alone with a sore pussy and aching thighs.

"You told me what you wanted to do to me," I said. "You said you were going to eat me out."

"Baby, I'm going to make a meal out of you. Now, be a good girl and hop in the back seat."

He didn't raise his voice. He hadn't raised his voice at any point during our encounter, not even when he squared off against Sergio. Owl spoke in these quiet, dulcet tones that would lure a child to sleep, or off the wooded path to Grandma's house.

I expected him to challenge me, to try to cajole me. He did neither. He waited silently. His dark eyes dared me to step inside. I could turn around and leave. I didn't think that he would stop me if I tried to go.

I looked again at his firm body, his broad chest. It was going to be nice to curl up into that chest later this night and more nights to come. I ducked into the car.

Once inside I scooted to the opposite door placing my heeled shoes on the floor. Owl crawled in and shut the door. His body took up any remaining space in the cramped back seat.

I reached up and grabbed his neck. In a move

that would've made any martial artist proud, Owl's hands snaked out and grabbed my wrists. His fingers entwined with mine and he put them behind my head. The move knocked my breath out, made my heart speed up.

When he spoke it was that soft, calm voice. "What did I say about kissing?"

There was a firmness behind his words that turned my intellectual brain to mush.

"Kissing is a messy business, Kira, and I don't do that with strangers."

I struggled to add meaning to those words. "But you're going to eat me out."

Owl grinned. "Pussy is a delicacy I don't pass up." He reached his hand under my skirt and traced the seam of my g-string. "Ohh," he purred as he traced my bare pubic area. "And it looks like you cleaned up for me."

I wasn't a fan of pubic hair and always kept it shaved off. Actually, I wasn't a fan of guys eating me out either. I'd always offer a different course instead. "Why don't you turn around so I can give you a little head? As a thank you for helping me out."

"Maybe." Owl rubbed his thumb over my bare pussy lips. "When I'm done."

I failed to stifle my sigh of frustration and turned

it into a moan of what I hoped sounded like pleasure. I writhed my hips to encourage him to get on with it. That storm was coming soon. I wanted to be inside, out of the shower, and in bed with him before it broke.

Owl moved aside the fabric that covered my pussy. I held my breath expecting dry friction over my vagina. But instead, his fingers slipped and slid between my folds. To my surprise there was wetness there. My gasp this time wasn't an act.

Owl brought his thumb back from under my skirt. He put it in his mouth and sucked. "Hmmm."

His groan rumbled through me. I watched his tongue flick out of his mouth and over his thick thumb. A throb reverberated through my core. I jerked, shocked at the sensation.

"You just passed my taste test, Kira."

Another throb went through me. This time it rose up my back and reached the top of my spine, straightening my shoulders on the leather of the car seat. It was the nicest thing a guy had said to me in a long time. I think I could really come to like this guy. I reached between us for his dick.

"Let me suck you off," I said. "I give really good head."

Owl smiled at me. "Me, too." He shoved away my hands and disappeared between my thighs.

I sighed again. Hopefully, he took it as a sigh of pleasure. In truth, it was a sigh of irritation.

Owl seemed like the type of guy that actually got girls off instead of bragging about how they made their pussies drip drop. He seemed like the type of guy that was gentleman enough to stay down there until a girl came. I groaned, but not in the good way. It was going to be a long night.

I spread my legs wide for him and settled down to begin my practiced orgasmic performance. I took advantage of his deep growl of pleasure to clear my throat to prepare my vocal cords for the high-pitched soprano I was about to sing for his benefit.

Owl didn't go directly for my clit. He played in the creases of my thighs. I tried to help him by rotating my hips to get him more center. I wanted to get this party started, and over with as quickly as possible. But he used his big hands to maneuver me back into place.

I gave up and called up my to-do list for tomorrow. I needed to get some school supplies to prep for finals, which were coming up soon. I began to compile a detailed list of what to get, and where to get it in my head as Owl nibbled on my left labia.

I couldn't remember if I had a box of notecards or if I needed to get a new box. I moaned again and thrusted my pussy absentmindedly into Owl's mouth. I'd just add notecards to the list and if I wound up with two boxes it was cool.

Owl flicked at my clit.

"Oh," I moaned low and long trying to recall which size paper clips I was low on.

He flicked again.

"Oh god, yes." I elongated the *yes* for an entire breath and clenched my thighs around his face. That always got them riled up and ready to plunge into my pussy.

Owl pulled away from me. He rested his chin on my pubic bone and stared up at me. "You in a rush, Kira?"

The question threw me. My shopping list fell to shreds in my head. I forgot which octave I'd left off in my moaning. Owl's eyes were bright, alert. Shouldn't he have only two brain cells in working order right now?

"It just feels so good," I said with the same bright smile I'd given Sergio twenty minutes ago. "I was almost there."

Owl raised that eyebrow again. "Were you now?"

It was a challenge, like he knew the truth; that I was faking it.

"Yeah," I lied. "What would really help me is if I could put your dick in my mouth. That really turns me on." And it would get him off and put him into a coma by the time I got him back to my place where I could rest easily against his warm body.

"He never got you off, did he?"

Fuck. Owl had more than a few brain cells working. He had complete control of his faculties.

No, Sergio had never gotten me off. No guy had ever gotten me off. Hell, I had never gotten off, period. I'd never experienced an orgasm in my life, but I wasn't about to tell Owl that. He looked like the type of guy who would take that as a challenge and I didn't have time to deal with his male ego. There was a storm coming, and I had a big bed to fill.

"I'm going to take care of you, Kira."

The words sailed into my being and fogged up my brain. My belly clenched and that tingling over my skin started up again. I couldn't help but hope that this one would be The One. That this one would last.

My head cleared when Owl inserted first one than two fingers into my pussy. I realized he was talking about taking care of my orgasm, not taking care of me as a person. Of course that was his goal. He was a guy. He had to prove his manhood, especially now that he knew that Sergio hadn't been man enough for the job. Owl was not going to stop until he got me to come.

I took another deep breath and got my mind ready to give a convincing performance.

Owl stroked his fingers in an upward motion. I breathed a sigh of relief. It was uncomfortable. Discomfort was a familiar thing to me when it came to sex. This I knew how to handle. I moaned again like his two-pronged stabbing was the greatest thing in the world.

"Oh yeah," I moaned. "Right there, baby."

Owl stroked faster.

"That's... that's..." I fell over my words as the motion of his fingers hit a spot. It didn't feel good, per se. It felt... it was hard to describe how it felt.

There was a heaviness building inside me, like I had to pee. I tried to squirm away from him, but he had my hips on lock down. I had to end this now before I embarrassed myself any further.

"Yes, yes." I called on my inner Meg Ryan. "Oh gawd, Owl. Awww." The performance would've won me an Oscar. I slumped back against the seat with a grin on my face.

Owl loomed over me. That same eyebrow rose as he peered down at me with an unconvinced face. My fake panting slowed. My sated grin faltered.

Owl leaned back down between my legs. He placed his fingers back inside me, not all the way, just up to the knuckles. He moved his fingers fast, faster. And then he added his tongue to my clit.

"Owl, what are you ahh..."

I jerked. A tremor started in my leg. The feeling of needing to pee intensified.

"Owl... wait... I'm gonna..."

It felt like my hips were being stacked with bricks of pressure. I bore down into the back seat of the car trying to release it, trying to get away from him. But he didn't stop. He wouldn't stop.

And then my body tensed, like the bricks that were weighing me down suddenly grew fingers. The fingers wrapped around me with that same amount of pressure, but they held me tight in a vice. They pressed into me, deep into me.

I couldn't speak. I couldn't breath. At any moment they were going to rip me apart. And then, I realized, I wanted to be ripped apart. I needed to be torn in two.

As soon as I came to that realization, as soon as my body was about to open up, Owl stopped.

THREE

Owl removed his tongue and his fingers from my pussy. My body trembled from the loss. I needed him to finish what he'd started, to break me open, and relieve all that pressure he'd built up inside me.

He pulled back from me and unbuckled his pants. He took out his dick. I'd been right in my estimation of his size. It was an impressive instrument, long and thick with a slight curve. He pulled a condom from his back pocket and tore it open with his teeth. He did all of this slowly, with absolutely no sense of urgency, while I lay writhing beneath him.

I was panting hard, whimpering. My body ached for his fingers to return, for his tongue to lick at my clit again. Had I been about to come?

I didn't want his dick. I didn't want him to pump

into me and bang away until he came. I wanted to come. And I half believed that I could.

But I couldn't ask him to go back to what he'd been doing before. I'd already pretended that I'd had my orgasm. And it looked like he knew it had been fake. That grin on his face as he placed the condom tip over his dick looked like he was teasing me.

"Oh, I almost forgot." He removed the unrolled condom from his dick, leaned back against the opposite door, and held his dick out. "Here you go," he said as he stroked the precum around the head. "Is this what you want, Kira? To suck me off?"

No, I wanted his face back between my thighs. I wanted his fingers hitting that spot. But I'd settle for this right now.

I was good at this; sucking dick. That's how I'd kept a man around for the last few years. I'd do this for him now, and maybe tomorrow night I'd get him to finger fuck me again. Maybe tomorrow night I'd have my first real orgasm with this quiet man with the intense eyes and magic hands.

I moved to get up. My knees wobbled as I put weight on them. My pussy felt like a weight hung from its center. I had to brace myself on the back of the driver's seat. Owl caught my upper body, a smirk on his face as he guided me down and onto his dick.

I gave him one last glance before I sank down into his lap. Now, it was my turn to smirk at him. He didn't know what he was in for.

I took hold of the base of his cock, holding it firm as I licked at the head. He was long with a nice girth. I'd seen my fair share of penises. It was easy to lead around the big, thick ones. But I preferred the small, skinny ones to be inside of me. They were no bother when they were in there. The thick ones always left me sore the next day.

I had planned to get Owl off quick, but I liked the feel of him on my lips, the taste of him on my tongue. Most girls I knew didn't like giving head. Most of the time I sided with them and their distaste of the act. It was a chore, but a necessary chore for a girl like me who wanted to keep a man around while she went off to the library to study. Every once in a while I found myself enjoying the chore.

I was enjoying myself with Owl. With the tip of my tongue I played with the veins along his dick. I licked at his balls, enjoying the shifting texture of his sack. He reached his hand down. I expected him to guide me fully onto his dick. But he didn't. He ran his fingers through my hair, gently, like a caress. I shuddered as they traced the cone of my ear.

I got down to business. I put him in my mouth,

working my tongue around his shaft. I relaxed my throat muscles and took him in deep, all the way to the back of my throat. There was still another inch or two of him that I couldn't fit.

Damn. He was the biggest dick I'd yet to encounter. I pulled out my whole bag of tricks.

I leaned my torso down, putting my ass in the air for him to admire.

I kissed at his length, using my words to compliment his impressive instrument.

I took him back in, sucking hard and making a pop when I withdrew.

I deep throated him, slobbering all over his length in the process.

Throughout my performance, Owl watched me with half lidded eyes. He didn't pump into my mouth. He didn't grab my ears or the back of my neck to keep me down there. He didn't impale himself up and into me. He relaxed back and let me do my thing.

His eyes never left me. That same soft smile on his face. His breathing was even. Long moments passed like this; him relaxed and me hard at work.

What the hell was happening? I'd always gotten guys off in less than five minutes -without fail. My jaw was becoming tired. I'd never jerked a guy off for this long without a result.

"Kira?" He reached down and lifted my mouth off his dick. "I want to fuck you now."

The head of his thick, long dick bounced off my chin. I looked at it. It curved in that same angle that his fingers did when they were inside me.

Maybe...?

Would I...?

Could I...?

I was throbbing between my thighs, aching to be filled by something. I'd been so close. Maybe he could get me there? Maybe he could get me to come?

I crawled over top of him. He slid his pants further down his thighs and rolled the condom on. He pushed my skirt up. He didn't bother removing my underwear, just kept the panties pushed to the side. He slowly impaled himself up and into me, allowing me to feel every inch of him. It should've hurt, but it was a welcome intrusion to my throbbing pussy.

Once he was all the way in, he stopped. He sat up with my knees spread wide over his thighs. He reached out and undid my shirt. With the buttons free, he pulled the garment down behind my back trapping my upper arms in the sleeves.

I couldn't move my upper body with my forearms trapped like that. I couldn't move my thighs with him inside of me. I was at his complete mercy.

He put us eye to eye and then he fucked up and into me. Not hard, but firm enough for me to feel every inch of him. Not slow, but fast enough to keep me panting. The moans came out of me unbidden. I felt that sweet pressure return. My eyes closed and my head lolled back.

"Kira."

I tried to give him my attention, but the pressure was collecting all around me.

"Kira, I don't want you to come."

His words made no sense. I must've imagined them in all of my haze.

I heard people coming around us, filling in the parking lot. Someone turned on an engine and music blared. I should care. I should tell Owl to stop, that someone might come close and see what we were doing, what he was doing to me. But I couldn't give them that much of my mind. It was all wrapped around Owl's dick and the magic it was working inside of me.

"Kira, you're gonna wait for me to come, and I'm not ready."

That was definitely Owl's calm voice, the calm

tinged with the firm command that had rankled me earlier. I'd listened to that commanding tone before, but I would not listen to it now.

Like hell I would wait.

I was so close. I'd never been this close in my entire life. I needed this. My thighs trembled. With one more thrust I'd be over this barrier.

Owl stopped and withdrew from me.

I felt like the world had been pulled out from under me. I felt like I'd been shoved off a cliff and was left flailing in the air, waiting for the impact of the ground to rend me into pieces. I felt like I'd been surfing on the tallest wave and crashed down into a wall of water that left my body stinging.

I could've screamed. Maybe I did scream. I couldn't move my arms, which were trapped in my blouse. I couldn't move my legs, which he had spread wide over his thighs.

I opened my eyes and glared at him.

Owl stared at me. His face transformed from calm amusement to displeasure. "I told you not to come, Kira."

The anger seeped from me as I looked at the displeased lines that gathered at the edges of his eyes. "I...I didn't," I panted.

Owl traced the lines of my lips, my chin. I

leaned into his touch like an eager kitten aching to be petted. A small smile broke over his mouth as he watched me. "But you want to. Don't you, Kira?"

What the fuck kind of mind games was this guy playing? I was frustrated and horny. I was on the verge of something I'd never experienced, something I thought other girls exaggerated about. And this guy was holding it from me, dangling it over my head while he laughed at me.

"Tell me you wanna come, Kira."

"What?"

"Beg me for it."

"You're an asshole."

Owl smiled. He dipped down and bit my breast through the lace of my bra.

I gasped. My legs shook. Something tightened in my core, but as it tightened I felt a fresh flush of wetness leak out of me.

"Mmm," Owl groaned. "Say it, and I'll give it to you." He reached down between us. He rubbed his thumb over my clit and then around my pussy lips where I'd dripped all over him. He stuck two fingers just inside my channel, coming just to the edge of that sweet spot.

He leaned back against the car seat. He stuck his fingers in his mouth, the fingers he'd just had in my wet, dripping pussy. I watched his tongue flicking over his digits. The throbbing increased in my pussy. I couldn't rub my thighs together because he had them spread wide. I couldn't touch myself because my hands were trapped. I would go out of my mind if I didn't get relief soon.

"Please, Owl. I'm begging you. This is me begging you."

Owl smiled. He grabbed his dick and thrust deep into me.

FOUR

But Owl didn't let me come right away. He continued to toy with me, thrusting fast and hard, and then slow and shallow.

"Fuck, you need it, baby. Don't you?"

"Please," I whimpered, no longer shamed at my neediness. I was already supplicating myself in his lap. My head bowed in reverence to the mastery he had over my pussy.

"Okay, baby. You wanna come?"

"Yes, please."

"Come for me, Kira."

And that was all it took.

It was better than I'd ever hoped it could be. It felt like I was in the movies. In those action scenes where time slows down.

I held on as Owl continued to stroke into me, slowly. I felt my body open up, like someone unlocking a door. I saw the key turning in the lock as the head of his penis pushed once more past my pussy lips. I heard the click as his dick filled me from my entrance all the way through to what felt like my belly.

That's when I knew I was going to come. But that wasn't the end. No, there was so much more.

Before my pussy clenched around him, his penis traveled back down the way it came, hitting every spot again. My heartbeat dropped; the rhythm slowed, and the beating descended into my pussy. I watched the door opening, heard it creaking wider and wider. I knew without a doubt that any minute it would be flung wide open and I would be knocked back.

It was an out of body experience. I sat high above myself, watching it all take place, suspended in the live animation of it all. And he was right there with me. Through the slowing of time, the turning of the lock, the opening of the door. At the exact moment that the door swung open, Owl grinned at me like he knew it was about to happen... right... now...

My body stiffened. My pussy seized and clamped around his thick cock, which was buried deep inside of me, as deep as he could push into me. The muscles inside my pussy felt like they contracted for an hour, and during that long wait for them to release I couldn't breathe . I couldn't move. I couldn't even think. I only saw him, grinning wide like a proud lion, eyes opened wide like his name-sake bird, taking it all in like it was beautiful, like I was beautiful.

I sighed and my body released. The sounds I made when I came were nothing like what I'd heard Meg Ryan doing in that movie. It was nothing like the canned cries of real porn stars. The sounds that came out of me were deep, guttural, helpless. Joyful.

When I stopped jerking, I collapsed against Owl, my face buried in the center of his chest

Owl pet my hair. "Good girl. That's better, isn't it?"

The self-preservation part of me knew I needed to get up off this dude and get as far away from him as possible. The amount of power and control he'd just exuded over not just my body, but my head as well, was more than any person ought to have over another human being. Plus, it was clear that he liked to play games. I didn't need another guy who would jerk me around.

But my body clamped itself around him. It wrapped itself around him and wouldn't let go. My arms, which had been freed sometime during or after my orgasm, were clasped around his biceps. My knees pressed into his thighs. He was still inside of me, not as hard as when I clenched around him during my orgasm, but still erect enough to stay inside me. My mind may have been saying run, but my body had other intentions.

"Hey Owl, you done in there?" Along with the voice from outside the car came a rap at the window.

The windows were tinted, but I could make out a large shadow. I jerked away from Owl, reaching for the ends of my shirt to cover myself. As I reached I felt my hips rooted to something, Owl's semi hard dick still buried deep inside of me.

"Relax," he said to me leaning back against the seat, making no move to remove his dick from my pussy. "It's just my boys."

His boys? Were they out there the whole time? We're they watching? I squirmed on top of him, trying to free myself from the anchor of his dick.

"You need some help in there?" said one of his boys.

Owl raised an eyebrow at me at the question. Then he chuckled at my reaction. He reached out his hands and freed me from his dick. "No we're good," he yelled to who ever was outside the car.

Owl's dick lay prone on his ripped lower abs. The purple condom glistened in the moon's light leaving tracks of my pussy juice at the edge of his navel. He patiently unfolded my arms from my breasts. He pulled my blouse back up and over my arms. He took his time fastening each button.

He reached between us and pulled the fabric of my underwear back over my pussy and straightened my skirt back over my still quivering legs. Then he motioned for me to climb off him so he could straighten himself out.

I sat huddled against the door watching him dispose of the condom and put his dick away with those magic fingers. My pussy, which felt like it had been opened for the first time, still sang his praises in a throbbing rhythm. Once Owl had himself put back together, he got out of the rear passenger door. He reached back in and held his hand out for me like a gentleman.

I stepped out of the car on shaky legs. Owl wrapped his other hand around my waist and held me steady.

"Fuck man, I see why you didn't want to share."

I looked over Owl's shoulder to see a bear of a man grinning down at me like I was a tasty morsel he wanted to pick his teeth with. He was flanked by two other men. Though not as big as him, they were both forces to be reckoned with. One was blond with the face of an angel, which let me know there had to be a devil hidden behind his dimpled cheeks. The other was a brother with a shiny, bald head.

"I'm gonna take her home," Owl said, opening the front passenger door and handing me inside. "I'll see you guys back at the house." He shut the door and went around to the driver's side. He started the car, and we were off.

"Did you have a good time?" His eyes were on the road as he asked. He asked the question as though we were talking about the weather.

"Were your friends there the whole time we were...?"

Owl shrugged. "I don't know? Probably not. They would've knocked on the window earlier and asked if you wanted them to join in."

"Join in?"

"Yeah." He didn't elaborate.

"So you guys do stuff like that? Share women?"

Owl turned to me with a smile. "Hey kettle,

don't call me black when you just went from your boyfriend's limp dick to the back seat of my car."

"My ex-boyfriend who was cheating on me."

Owl shrugged. "I only saw a man talking to another girl."

"He was all over her."

Owl shrugged again. "I don't understand the whole boyfriend/girlfriend/monogamy thing. Cheating, to me, is when you take advantage of a girl. Like getting a girl to blow you and not returning the favor. Now, that would be a dick move to get pissed about."

I looked at him like he was crazy. Because that statement, that definition, was crazy.

Owl looked over at me and grinned. "I get it. You're a mono girl. You believe in monogamy."

A crack of thunder sounded from outside the car. "You don't?"

"I don't think it's fiction. I've seen it work for some people, like my parents. I just have no interest in it personally. But you do, don't you Kira. I should probably tell you to stay away from me."

I had planned to stay away from him. People tell you who they are when you meet them. My problem was that I rarely listened.

"But I won't tell you that," Owl said. "I enjoyed fucking you tonight. I'd like to do it again."

My pussy throbbed at the prospect. "I just got out of a relationship. I'm not ready to play any more games."

"Did you hear a word I said? I don't want a relationship with you. I want to fuck you. And trust me, you'd like the games I'd play with you."

He stopped the car. I looked out the window. We'd arrived at my dorm. Owl hopped out of the car and came around to my door. He helped me out and handed me a card. "Watchers Auto and Body," the card read. At the top it had a tire with wings over the lettering.

"Give me a call if you want another ride, Kira. I'd be more than happy to come and get you."

"You're not gonna come up?"

"What for? It's late. I'm tired. I'm gonna head home and get some sleep. I hope you call, Kira." And with that, he took off into the night.

Up in the sky, the storm clouds were rolling away. They'd never even broken. I looked down at the card in my hand. I should leave it on the pavement. This guy wasn't boyfriend material. He didn't believe in monogamy. He'd said he liked fucking women and sharing them with his boys. This was definitely not the kind of relationship I needed in my life.

I stood outside for long moments twirling the card between my fingers. Finally, I turned towards my dorm. With each step I took my pussy throbbed at the absence of Owl buried deep inside of me. For the first time, it wasn't a painful ache. It was twinges of longing. I held the card in the palm of my hand and made my way inside.

When I got to my door, Sergio was there waiting.

"What are you doing here?" I said.

"I wanna talk," he said.

Even from far away, I spotted the pink lipstick on the collar of his shirt. I shook my head. "I don't want to talk to you."

"Did you fuck him? That yellow chin-?"

"You're a racist asshole. And your ignorant as well because he's Japanese, not Chinese...I think. And yeah, I did fuck him. And it was a good fuck. A really good fuck."

Sergio's face went beet red. "Well, I fucked that blonde too."

"Good for you." I shrugged, turning the key into the lock of my door. I felt another twinge in my pussy at the sound, reminding me of Owl unlocking my orgasm.

"Wait, Kira. You don't want me to come in? You gonna send me out into the night? There's a storm coming."

"The storm already passed, Sergio." I went in and closed the door in his face.

I took out Owl's card. I programmed the number into my phone. But instead of hitting Save, I hit Talk.

The phone rang.

I panicked.

Before I could hang up, he answered. "Hello?"

I gulped. "Hey, Owl. I was just putting your number in my phone and hit Talk instead of Save and-"

"You in your room?"

"Y-Yes."

"Me, too."

"You got home fast."

He chuckled. "I drive a race car. You alone?"

"Yeah."

"Me, too. Take off your panties."

My hand shook as I held the phone to my cheek. It felt like I was about to cross some invisible line.

"Kira," there was steel in his soft, calm voice. "Take off your panties and go lay down on your bed."

My feet moved to the beat of my throbbing pussy. The bed creaked under my weight as I sat down.

"Good girl," he said. "Put your fingers in your mouth. Get them good and wet."

He waited while I did as he asked.

"Now, spread your thighs..."

FIVE

"Make big, slow circles around your clit, Kira."

The sound of Owl's voice in my ear sent shivers across my shoulder blades. I was hot, burning up all over. I tilted my head back and sweat ran down my brow. My chin slipped against the cool plastic of the phone. The temperature difference made me gasp.

"I said slow, Shakira."

"I am," I whimpered.

I wasn't. My index finger skated erratic figure eights over my throbbing clit. The only thing slowing the digit down was the sticky, wet mess I'd made. The sound of Owl's quiet commands, mixed with the sappy stirrings of me scrubbing that bundle of nerves were about to send me over.

"Slow down." His words were no louder than a

whisper. "I want you to come long and hard for me, baby."

With the pad of my finger, I started a slow trip around the top of my clit, but by the time I got to the bottom, I'd picked up speed.

"If you keep rubbing that little pearl of yours fast, you'll come."

God yes, that's exactly what I wanted to do.

"It'll be over just as soon as it began," his tone tsked a warning. "Is that what you want? To come and be done?"

Um yeah, that's exactly what I wanted to do. What more was there?

"I can make you come all night, Kira. I can make it last longer. I can make you come harder. Would you like that, baby?"

My finger slowed after his clarification. My hand shook in the wake of his promise. My entire body felt pulled as taut as an arrow in the catch of a bow, just waiting for Owl to release his trigger finger and shoot me long and far.

"Good girl."

There was rustling on his end of the line, like he was adjusting himself in his bed. I wondered if he was touching himself as he told me where, and how, and how fast to touch myself. I'd tried to reciprocate, to talk dirty to him, but he always steered the conversation back to me and my pussy.

We'd been at this for a week now. He'd call every night just before midnight. He didn't immediately launch into phone sex. He'd ask me about my day, my classes, my thoughts. He listened with interest. He asked probing questions. He followed up on subjects we'd talked about days before making me believe he'd actually listened to and thought about what I'd said in previous conversations. If he were trying to seduce me, just these conversations alone would've done the trick. I'd have let him in my panties; let him put it anywhere he wanted to, just for all that attention.

I'd started touching myself during these talks, way before he'd tell me to take my panties off and spread my legs for him. I'd listen to his voice as he spoke about his recent trip with his parents to Japan, or about the new part he'd gotten for his car, or about some joke his buddy Crow had told the other day. I'd listen with open ears, soaking up every detail of his life and cataloguing it for future use when I'd claim the label of girlfriend. I let his dulcet tones wash over me and, before I knew what they were doing, my fingers were in my panties and all over my swollen pussy.

Owl knew what I was doing. He always seemed to know every move I'd planned to make, every thought I was about to say, before I knew myself. Every time I'd touch myself before he told me to, he'd launch into a long story about a new car on the market or an antique model he was trying to repair; things he knew I had absolutely no interest in or understanding of. But he'd talk until I started to pant, and then finally, he'd take over directing my touches.

I'd been right. Owl liked to play games. But he'd been right, too. I liked his games.

"Is it sticky, Kira? Let me hear it. Put the phone on speaker and then put it on your belly."

I obeyed without a second thought. The sounds of my fingers running through my dripping pussy filled the air alongside Owl's groans of appreciation.

"That's it, baby. Nice and slow."

"Owl, please. I want to come."

"I know you do, baby. I'm going to get you there."

I'd never been one to masturbate. I'd tried when I was younger, but it never worked for me. It just wound up being a frustrating time-suck.

For the past week I'd come every single night with Owl. After we'd hang up, I'd lay in bed with my pussy throbbing in that good way of being satisfied from proper use. I'd fall asleep with my phone clutched inside my curled up hand, which would be pressed against my cheek or my heart. I'd wake up every morning aching for Owl's arms around me, for that warm body heat next to me. I'd spend all day watching the clock, counting down the minutes, until he'd call and fuck me over the phone again.

"You're close, aren't you, Kira?"

"I want... I want..."

"Tell me what you want, baby."

"I want you."

Owl let out a sound that reminded me of a purring lion looking out over his pride. Lion males typically had around five females in their cluster. Owl had told me on that first night that he didn't believe in monogamy. Once or twice I'd heard a woman call to him in the background. I knew I wasn't the only one. I couldn't be.

But the fuck if I didn't want to be. I just needed to get him here with me. Once he was here, I could find a way to be his number one. And then, his one and only.

"I want you inside me, Owl."

"Soon, baby."

"I want to come. I want it so bad. When you

were inside me I came so hard. I want that again. Come over here and give that to me, Owl. Please."

"Stop," he said. "Stop touching yourself right now, Kira."

He'd put base in his voice. There was force behind his words. He wasn't yelling at me, but it felt like an admonishment.

I pulled my hand away and struck my pillow with a clenched fist. My orgasmic high evaporated like rain drops in the sun. My bliss turned to frustration. "What the fuck do you want from me?"

"I want to make you feel good, Kira."

"Then come over and fuck me," I snapped, letting my blue clit get the better of me.

Owl didn't respond. He did that a lot. Whenever I asked him to come over, to let me come to him, to meet somewhere out in public, he redirected the conversation or simply clammed up.

I picked up the phone from my belly and put it back to my ear. "If you have a girlfriend, just say so."

"I don't have a girlfriend," he said. "I told you that when we first met. I don't tell lies. They're too complicated to remember, and I like things to be simple."

"Then why are you doing this to me? Why won't you come and see me?"

"Because you have no control over your orgasms, Shakira. You'd come as soon as I entered you and that won't satisfy me. I'm helping you learn release control before I fuck you again."

Control over my orgasms? Release control? What the fuck did that even mean? "I don't know what you're talking about? I've never had *any* orgasms before you."

"Wait." There was more rustling on his end of the line, like he was rising to sitting from a prone position on his bed. "Not even before limp dick Sergio?"

I rose too, folding my legs underneath my ass to assuage my throbbing, needy pussy. "No," I went with the truth. I'd already begged this guy to come over and fuck me, what more did I have to lose. "No guy has ever made me come."

"You've played with yourself though? You've gotten yourself off? Right?"

There was a break in his voice. That note of incredulity lit a spark of hope in my chest. Maybe more of the truth would get him over to my doorstep and inside my yearning pussy.

"I've never been able to make myself come, either. Even now, without your voice telling me what to do, I can't do it on my own. You're the only guy who's ever gotten me there."

I could've heard a pin drop on the other end of the line. Even his breath was silent, or maybe he'd stopped breathing all together.

"I can't make myself come," I continued. "I've never been able to. I've never been able to get off with a guy either. I've always faked it. You're the only one who's ever gotten me off, and you like to play these games with me. It fucking sucks."

There was still silence on the other end of the line.

"Owl?"

I thought maybe he'd hung up on me. He probably had. Who wanted a girl who couldn't come? A girl who faked it. I'd pretended to like sex for so long, only because it would get me what I wanted; a warm body laying in bed next to me.

I hated being alone. There, I admitted it. I was smart, pretty, and independent. I'd gotten a full academic scholarship to college, kept high marks in all my classes, and was a clear favorite at the urban planning firm where I worked part time. The one area of my life I did not excel at was in the relationship department. No matter what I did, I couldn't seem to hold onto a man. And at the end of the day that was the thing I wanted most; to be in a committed relationship.

For the longest time, sex was the only currency that seemed to pay off in that endeavor. Now, with Owl, was the first time I'd gotten anything back from the investment. That return on investment had turned my world upside down. I hadn't known that sex could be satisfying for both parties. And now that I was getting paid, I didn't want to be broke again.

"Owl, are you still there?"

"I'll be right over." He hung up the phone.

SIX

Owl knocked on the door ten minutes later. I'd barely had time to catch my breath and cover myself. I'd put on a silk robe and was bare beneath it. My body was far too sensitized to deal with fabric directly on my skin. The soft silk running over my nipples set my knees to quaking, but I was able to make my way to the door.

He stood in the doorway in a linen shirt and dark jeans. Those almond-shaped eyes peered down at me, narrowing to slits as he took in my skimpy wardrobe. With one hand, he swept his dark locks out of his eyes. With the other hand he took the doorjamb from my hands. He opened my door wide to allow him a clear, unobstructed view of me.

"How did you get here so fast?" My voice was breathless as I stood there in my flimsy robe.

The hall was mostly empty. The few girls that were headed to or headed out of their rooms paused mid stride, staring at us. Not at us. They were all staring at him.

"I drive a fast car." Owl leaned against the door-jamb. "Invite me in."

I suddenly felt like I was one of those vapid heroines in romance novels, the ones that didn't make a move without the sparkly vampire or angsty werewolf giving them permission. "You can't come in without my permission? What are you a vampire?"

Owl grinned. "This is the only time tonight I will give you a choice. And when you let me in..." His eyes dipped down to my hips as though he saw my throbbing clit through the silk robe covering it. "... I will suck you dry."

The intensity in his eyes should've scared me. But it didn't. This was what I'd been wanting all week. For him to come and put his hands on me instead of telling me what to do.

He was here. He was with me. And by the end of the night, I'd treat him so good he'd want to stay.

I stepped aside with a wide grin of my own. Owl

came into the room. I arched my head up as he passed, but he didn't offer me a kiss. Of course he didn't. I remembered what he'd said about kissing; that it was less hygienic than oral sex.

Well, that was okay, for now. If he didn't want the lips on my face, I'd happily spread my thighs for him to get at the other pair of lips that ached for him.

I watched Owl as he took stock of my dorm room. "You a neat freak, Kira?"

My desk was clear and tidy. The books were stacked upright by height and width. I had one cup of pencils that were all the same height. Another cup of pens were divided evenly between black and blue ink. I'll admit, my need for order might be a little OCD. But when things were easily within my reach, I could move about my day efficiently.

I reached for Owl. He caught my hand before I touched him. I noticed that his shirt was perfectly starched. The disheveled look of his hair was by no accident. Each wayward strand of hair seemed trimmed and teased to fall at the precise, messy angle.

"Take your robe off, Kira."

I hesitated. I'd planned on running this rodeo, telling him to get naked so I could take out that thick cock and use my mouth to stake my claim. I supposed that could wait awhile. He owed me an orgasm.

I undid the knot and let the robe slide to the floor.

Owl sat down in my desk chair and surveyed my body. My nipples pebbled into tight points under his gaze. My pussy started a slow, pounding rhythm.

"Did you come?"

"No," I said parting my thighs. "I told you I couldn't. Not without you."

Something passed over his face. I couldn't determine exactly what it was, but it made the beating between my thighs speed up.

"Come here, Kira."

I came and stood between his thighs.

"On your knees."

I frowned, putting my brown hands on my full hips. "We are not going to make this some Master/slave fantasy. I am not gonna play your little servant."

Owl leaned back in the chair. "You got it wrong, baby. I'm here to serve you." He sat back and waited for me to comply.

I squirmed under his dark eyes. The man had the patience of a turtle. The throbbing in my pussy increased, going from a slow march to the upbeat drumming of a rock song. I'd already learned that my orgasms were shy without the voice or presence of Owl.

"Fine." I allowed my knees to buckle and went down slowly to the floor.

Owl smiled a triumphant grin. Slowly, he leaned forward. He took my face in his hand. "You been fucking anybody else?"

"No," I said. "Have you?"

"Mmm hmm."

I pulled back from his touch. I don't know what shocked me more? That I'd been right about him fucking other women, or that he confirmed it so nonchalantly.

Owl stared at me. "If you don't want honesty, don't ask."

I tensed my jaw.

"I fucked four girls this week," he said.

He reached over and picked up one of my blue pens. He twirled it in his fingers and then placed it on the right side of the cup with the black pens. My eyes flew from the chaos of the pens back to his dark eyes. I made to get up, to right the order of my pens, but Owl stayed me with his hand. It was a gentle gesture, but my body obeyed under his touch.

"While I was fucking them," he said, "after I

fucked them, sometimes before I fucked them, I thought about making you come. I can't stop thinking about making you come." He moved the blue pen back over with the other blues. "That was the first time you came, wasn't it? That first night with me?"

I looked away, not responding.

"And you've never made yourself come on your own? Just with me?"

He ran his thumb over my lip. The back and forth movement was hypnotic. My clit throbbed in time to it. He leaned in towards me. I thought he would kiss me. But he pulled his hand away and reached into his pocket.

"I brought you a present."

Owl pulled out a box. He didn't hand it to me. He opened the package himself. What he pulled out of the packaging made me catch my breath. It was a pink egg with a wire and remote coming off one end. I'd never used one before, but I knew what it was.

"Spread your thighs for me, Kira."

I opened my mouth to question him, but I didn't get any words out. I felt the condensation pool around my pussy as he toyed with the vibrator. I closed my mouth and opened my thighs for him.

He reached to my pussy. His fingers spread my

pussy lips. The sap that gathered there was loud as my juicy lips separated. I could've imagined it, but I swore I heard a slurping sound as Owl pushed the cold piece of metal into my pussy. His thumb swiped my clit before he sat back in the chair.

He leaned back with the controls in his hand. "I'm going to turn this on. You're not to come, do you understand?"

"Wait. What? Why not?"

Owl raised an eyebrow at me. "Because I said so."

"You told me you would make me come."

"And I will."

I opened my mouth to protest again, but he turned the dial on and the buzzing started. I reached out and grabbed his knee.

It felt like one of those church bells ringing inside of me. Only the metal stick thing that made the bell vibrate was dinging at twenty times the speed. The bell didn't sway so much as shake my core. It shook so fast that my teeth rattled. On its own, my pussy muscles clenched around the ringing vibrator.

"Shakira," Owl took my chin between his fingers. I smelled myself on his thumb. "You will hold this in you for five minutes. And you are not going to come while it's in there."

"Owl... please..."

"Oh baby, I'm going to give you what you need, I promise. I'm going to make it so good. But you have to do what I say first. Trust me, Kira. You trust me?"

Did I? I'd never trusted a man to do anything but lie and cheat. They'd all lied to me. They'd all cheated on me. They'd all left me.

Owl planted feather light kisses on my brow. "Trust me, Kira. I just want to please you. Three and a half minutes to go."

I felt the orgasm building inside me. My pussy muscles continued to tremble and weep more fluid. The muscles were hungry. They suckled at the vibe, like the draws lips make when sucking on a lollipop.

I took a deep breath. It didn't help. The sensation didn't subside, it increased. But, I didn't come.

"Good girl," Owl kissed my chin. "Two minutes."

The pressure was becoming unbearable. I clutched at him, unable to form words as I concentrated on not munching down on the juicy sucker inside of me to get to the bliss-filled center.

"Don't come, baby. Hold it for me. Wait for me, Kira."

Owl kissed around my eyelids, so gently. My body and head felt disconnected from each other as they both screamed for different things.

"You ready, baby?"

I was ready to give him anything he wanted. I felt him wrench the vibrator out of me. I was airborne and then on the bed. I felt him unbuckle his pants. There was the crinkle of a condom wrapper. And then he was inside me. He threw my legs over his shoulders and pumped into me hard and fast.

"Come for me, Kira."

And I did. Just like that my body erupted. Owl held me tight. When my body stopped shaking I felt something crash into my mouth. Owl's lips were on me, his tongue invading me.

He flipped me over and on to my belly. He was back inside of me before I could catch my breath. He pumped rhythmically, his dick the new gong making my bell ring.

"Come for me, Kira."

Barely finished with the first orgasmic clenching, my body obeyed for a second time. These contractions weren't as strong, but they still knocked the wind out of me. When they stopped Owl pulled out. He turned me back over and onto my back. He spread my thighs and put his face in my pussy.

I tried to close my legs. "Owl, I can't. I'm too sensitive."

"Yes, you can."

He coaxed my thighs back open. I didn't have the mental or physical power to stop him.

He licked at me once, just once. A long, slow, slurp. "Give it to me, Kira. Come for me."

I felt like my body was a rag twisting the last bit of water from its cloth as a third orgasm tore through my center. When I regained consciousness, Owl's head lay against my thigh. His eyes were on me, owl-wide. He wasn't smiling.

"I need to go." He got up, pulled off the used condom, and began putting his clothes back on.

My head was foggy, my body heavy, but I scrambled up after him. "Why?"

"Shhh, baby." He paused in buttoning up his jeans. He leaned down and planted a kiss along my forehead, over my brow, on my eyelids. "I'll be back tomorrow night."

"Why don't you stay tonight?"

He looked at my bed. "I don't sleep well in strange beds."

"Want me to come with you?" I know my voice sounded needy, but I couldn't help it.

Owl knelt down until his face was on my level.

"I don't sleep well with someone else in my bed. I'll be back tomorrow. In the meantime, I want you to use this in the morning."

He handed me the vibrator and the controller.

"I want you to hold it in yourself for five minutes. When you do, I do not want you to come. You need to learn control over your releases because I plan to fuck you for longer than an hour the next time."

I looked over at the clock. It was well beyond 2am. He'd gotten here shortly after one.

"Use it three times a day and don't come. I'll see you tomorrow night." He kissed me again, this time a light kiss on the lips with a quick swipe of his tongue.

And then he was gone.

SEVEN

After Owl left the previous night, I was out like a light in twenty minutes. These orgasms were doing wonders for my sleep issues. I woke up in the morning with a throbbing clit that begged for attention. This morning, instead of reaching out for a man, I reached for the gift Owl left for me.

I set my timer with my phone and then I placed the vibrator inside me. There was tenderness in my pussy from where Owl had thrust in and pulled out three orgasms the night before. It was a good tenderness and my pussy lips clenched around the metal egg.

I turned up the dial and immediately dropped the control. I had to dig my nails into the mattress to stop myself from immediately coming. I took a deep breath to calm myself down, but my body stayed on that tight rope that hovered above the descent into orgasmic bliss.

Clutching at the mattress, breathing deep, neither worked. My body stayed balanced precariously on the tight rope. I didn't fall off the rope into an orgasm, but neither did I gain a strong foothold on the rope. I hovered in that space right before the fall.

A beeping noise brought me back to my senses. It was the timer. I couldn't believe it had already been five minutes. With shaky hands I gave a tug to the wire connecting the egg to the controls. It came out of me with a juicy pop.

I lay back on the bed grinning from ear to ear, anticipating revisiting the egg for lunch, and then again at dinner, and then having Owl inside me for dessert tonight. I left my room with a pep in my step and headed over to the biology lab for my tutoring session.

"Good morning, Shakira."

"Hey, sis." My tutor Ellie was the whitest, white girl I'd met on the campus. But even her awkward quirkiness couldn't distract me today.

Although I was in the School of Architecture studying Urban Planning, I still had a biology requirement. It was the only class I had a B in. Science was not my strong suit.

Evolution and Natural Selection were giving me a problem. That problem was with Darwin's Theory of Super Fecundity. Darwin saw that organisms produced more offspring than is required to replace themselves. Based on this it would follow that population sizes would increase rapidly.

"And when that happens," said Ellie, "we may need to share our resources more efficiently. Food, water, shelter, mates."

"Mates? You think God intended us to share mates? You can't be serious, sis."

Ellie shrugged. "It works in the animal world."

"Maybe for the males."

"Actually for females, too," Ellie insisted. "There are many matriarchal societies in the insect world. Take bees for instance. One queen to mate all the male drones."

"That's what we'd call a whore in human society."

Ellie shrugged again. "Most queens live very satisfied lives while her female workers never see any male attention. I doubt the queen would care what any of them thought about her." Ellie looked off to the bee enclosure with a far off look in her eyes.

I went back to my notes.

The buzzing in my pocket made me jump in my seat. For a moment, I worried that I'd left the vibe inside me. But it was just my phone vibrating in my pocket. I looked down at the caller ID.

"I have to take this," I said gathering my papers and shoving them haphazardly into my otherwise organized bag.

"It's fine," Ellie said. "We were done for the day anyway. Same time tomorrow?"

"Yeah, thanks Ellie." I dashed out of the lab and hit Talk. "Hey."

"Where are you?" Owl's quiet voice was full of that commanding tone.

"I'm just leaving the biology lab."

"You're headed back to your room?"

"Yeah," I said. "I was going to use the present you gave me."

"You used it this morning?"

"Yes."

"Did you come?"

"No."

"Good girl. I want you to get to your room quickly. Take off all of your clothes and then shove the vibrator up that sweet pussy of yours."

"You could at least say please, you know."

"No, you're the one that says please, Shakira. You're the one that will be on her knees begging. Because you want it, don't you, baby? You needed it."

"I..."

"Hurry home, Kira. There are things I want to do to you. Things that will take time."

I picked up my pace.

"I want you dripping for me by tonight, Kira. I want you aching for me to fill up that pussy."

I took off at a run. I was panting by the time I got to my door while Owl kept telling me the filthy things he would do to me.

I'd never begged a man. I'd never let one tell me what to do. I usually was the one with the balls in the relationship because I usually licked the guy's testicles into submission. And then I'd hold his balls in a vice grip until, inevitably, they left me to go sniff up some other girl's skirt.

Not today. I'd made a decision. I'd follow Owl in this aspect of my life, my sex life. He obviously knew what he was doing. He'd taken me to places I didn't know existed inside the bedroom, in the back seat of a car. And he had yet to lead me astray.

I got into my room. I undressed, and I grabbed the vibe.

"Lay down," he commanded. "Put the phone on speaker. I want to hear you put my present inside you."

The stickiness of my dripping pussy and the buzzing of the vibe were the only sounds in the room. That and Owl's groans of appreciation.

"Don't close your legs," he commanded.

I swear it was as though he could see me. He anticipated my every move, my every desire, before I was even aware I wanted it. I needed the friction of pressing my thighs together, but I did as he said. I reached my heels to each corner at the bottom of the bed.

"You laying down, Kira?"

"Yes, Owl."

"Good girl. Stretch your hands over your head and hold onto the headboard."

I did as he said. I spread my legs wide on the bed and stretched my hands over my head. I felt completely exposed.

"Stay like that and do not come. Do you understand me, Kira?"

"Mmm hmm." But I already felt the sensations building in me.

"I didn't understand you, Shakira."

Part of my brain wanted to rail against the bass

in his voice, but the rest of me craved it. "Yes, Owl. Yes, I understand."

"That's my girl."

God, that's what I wanted. To be his girl.

"You remember the first time I had my tongue on you?" he asked. "You acted like it didn't affect you. Maybe it didn't. But now if I swirled my tongue over your clit it would jump for me wouldn't it?"

"Yes, yes." My clit jumped at the memory of his velvet tongue against me. It wept at the sound of his voice suggesting a repeat visit.

"If I licked open your pussy lips I'd find them plump and soaking wet, wouldn't I, Kira? I could lick my tongue up the sides and you'd get juicier and juicier, wouldn't you baby?"

"Oh god, yes." I felt the juices spilling out of me, running down the crack of my ass.

"Then I could put my tongue right inside you and taste all that sweet juice as it came down."

"Owl, stop. Please. I'm gonna come."

"Did I say you could come?"

"Please, Owl. Please."

"Not yet, baby."

"I can't stop. I can't stop."

"Shakira."

His voice resonated through me, stronger than

the impending contractions. My entire world came to a stop.

"Turn off the vibe, Kira."

"No, please don't ask me to do that. I need it." I was whining like a child about to have their new toy taken away.

"Take it out."

I had no intention of doing as he asked, but somehow I uncurled my fingers from the headboard. I reached down between my spread thighs and gave the cord connecting the vibe a yank. I was so wet it slid easily out of my pussy.

"Is it out?"

"Yes." I hoped he heard the pissy pout in my voice.

"Did you come?"

"No."

"Good girl."

And then he hung up the phone.

I was so sensitized, so achy, so needy. I started to cry.

What the fuck? What had I gotten myself into?

Fuck this. I reached my hand between my legs and rubbed. I was so swollen and wet. But the more I rubbed the drier I got.

I put the vibe back in and turned it on. It lay

nestled in my needy pussy, ringing its bell at high speeds. But I still couldn't come.

I lay there for ten minutes with it inside of me. I stayed there on the edge of oblivion with no way down. I needed Owl. I needed his voice or his presence to sail off this cliff that held me prisoner. I nearly reached out for my phone, but I didn't. I pulled out the vibe and curled into a fetal position instead.

EIGHT

Ten minutes later there was a knock on my door. I didn't move.

"Kira?"

My body responded to his voice. My nipples, which had been soft in the cool afternoon air, hardened. My clit, which had been quietly pulsing, pounded a harsh rhythm. But I refused to move.

"Kira, let me in."

I dug my fingers into the mattress.

"I'll make it better, baby. I promise."

Slowly, I unfurled myself from the bed. I didn't even bother to cover myself. I opened the door bare ass naked. Owl stood on the other side. He glanced down at my body, and then he opened his arms.

"Come here, baby."

And like a traitor, I went to him. He scooped me up and brought me inside, closing the door behind us. He lay down on the bed and brought me into his chest. He stroked my bare ass and my back, soothing me like a mother would an upset child. But I was a grown ass woman, and so I tried to hitch my leg over his thigh to get at his genitals. He brought my leg down and tucked my knees between his legs.

"Shh," he tried to hush away my horniness, but my hormones were raging.

"Why won't you let me come?"

"I will always make you come, baby. But you need to learn to get control of yourself first. You're completely focused on orgasming. Sex is about more than just coming. I want to show you how much higher I can take you."

"I don't understand you."

"I know, baby. But I need you to trust me."

I sighed.

Owl rolled me underneath him. "One thing you need to know about me, Kira, is that I'm a man of my word. I say what I mean, and I do what I say."

"I have trouble believing that."

"That's because you've been fucking shit-for-men that lie to get what they want. I've told you exactly what I want. And I've always given you what you need."

He stroked his hand up and down my body. I buried my face in his chest and took a whiff. He smelled like a woman's perfume.

"Where were you tonight?"

"At a party." His eyes challenged mine to ask the question I really wanted to know.

"Did you..." I hesitated because I knew he would tell me the truth, and I wasn't sure I wanted to hear it.

"Why is it important to you to know who I fuck as long as I come back to you every night?"

I closed my eyes. So he had come from fucking another girl.

"I didn't fuck anybody, Shakira. I watched two girls fuck each other, but I didn't touch either one of them."

"Why did you have to watch them? Why didn't you just come here and fuck me?"

He thought about that as he stroked my leg. "Why do you change your clothes every day? Why do you eat different foods at each meal? Why do you need more than one color pen to do your work? Just like food, clothes, and shelter, fucking is a basic necessity of human existence. We might wear the same outfit more than once, or have a favorite food, but we like variety."

"So you're saying I'm your favorite because you want to come and fuck me more than once?"

"Why do you need me to make you feel special? What if I change my mind about you one day? Does that mean you're not special anymore?"

Yeah, that's exactly what it meant. All the men who'd left me behind in the past; all the men I couldn't hold on to, that's why they all left.

"I'm not that guy, Shakira. I don't ride horses or wear tights, or any of that shit. I'm not from a story-book or samurai fairytale. I'm from Jersey."

I burst out laughing.

Owl grinned. "Just let me fuck you, baby. Let me make you come until you cry. That's what you need. And that's what I want to give you."

That was what I needed right now. I spread my legs and grabbed a hold of the headboard.

"That's my girl."

I let go of the headboard and put my hand up. "Owl, you're gonna have to stop calling me that. It messes with my head."

"Calling you what?" He reached out a hand and tweaked one of my breasts.

I took a deep breath before I continued. "Your girl. I'm not your girl."

He didn't answer. He reached for the other breast.

"I'm not," I said. "Am I?"

With his other hand Owl reached between us and put his fingers in me. "How about this? This is my pussy." He stroked up with his index and middle finger hitting that good-good spot. He stroked my clit with his thumb.

My legs opened wider for him. "Yeah, it's your pussy, Owl."

He smiled at that, like a little boy that just got a toy car. "Yeah, that's my pussy. I'm gonna make my pussy come. I'm gonna make my pussy drip."

My hips moved in time to his finger thrusts. I was close in less than a minute. But then he withdrew.

"Owl, what the fuck?"

"It's dripping," he said. "I wanna taste it."

I slapped my legs closed. He raised an eyebrow at me. I tried to mimic the gesture, but felt both of my brows raise to my hairline instead of just one. "You want a taste? I want a taste to." I indicated his crotch.

He smirked. "You want it?" He grabbed my legs

and flipped me over so that I was on top of him with my pussy over his mouth. "Go get it baby."

Owl pulled my hips down to his tongue and took a slurping lick. My upper body crumbled, and I fell face first into his crotch. He chuckled. His breath tickled my clit making it throb even more.

I reached for his belt to get at his cock, but he parted my ass cheeks and rimmed my asshole. My upper body collapsed at the first feel of those new sensations. I'd had a few boyfriends who I'd engaged in anal sex with. But they all had simply slapped on a condom, applied lubrication, and got down to the messy business of ass fucking. I'd never enjoyed it, not once. It always left me sore and dreading the toilet for days after. No one had ever taken their tongue there before.

Owl licked at my anus just like he would my clit. First light flicks, then wet circles, and then finally he sucked. I was trembling and moaning. Getting to his dick was a distant memory.

He spread my cheeks wide, dragging his tongue from my anus all the way back to my clit. He'd focus alternately on my clit, then my anus with those flicks, circles, and sucks. As soon as I could predict his motions, he changed them up. He let my ass cheeks go and spread my pussy lips. He stuck his tongue up my channel, lightly nipping with his teeth.

My mission to suck his cock dry was completely abandoned now. I lay my head beside his dick, which was still covered in jeans. I felt it twitching. Was it laughing at my sub par attempts to bend its owner to my will?

Owl didn't urge me to unzip him and get to work on his dick. In fact, with the few brain cells I had left, I was certain he'd rimmed my ass to get me to lose my focus. It was as though he was content to spend the whole night pleasing me.

But that was absurd. No guy was that selfless.

I rallied my senses and unzipped his pants. His dick spilled out, standing at the ready. I got to work kissing at the swollen head. I'd had many cocks in my day, but there was something pleasing about the texture and taste of Owl's. I licked up the precum in the divot of his cockhead. Then I suckled the underside of the bulbous head, reveling in the curves and how they fit perfectly in the cradle of my tongue.

Still, Owl didn't urge me on. He didn't reach up and grab my head to push me all the way down on him. He didn't thrust up into my mouth to force me to take more of him. He lay perfectly still from the torso down and let me have my way with him. From the torso up was a different story.

He inserted one finger into my pussy. That finger made a hook and hung out there while he licked at the soft patch of skin between my anus and vagina. I'd never known that that area had any pleasure nerves. Owl obviously did because he took his time playing there. I felt myself getting wetter and wetter as he stroked with his finger and tongue.

I refused to be the only one slowly going out of their mind. I took his whole cock in my mouth, relaxing my throat muscles to accommodate his length and girth. It was a mistake. It appeared to be exactly what he was waiting for me to do.

As soon as I reached the base of his cock, Owl inserted another finger into my pussy. With two fingers he pressed down and into the front of my vaginal wall, hitting what I now knew was my G-spot. I whimpered and gurgled on his dick. He chuckled as his mouth moved over my clit.

He'd made this a competition; the oral sex Olympics. I was clearly about to take the silver medal while he'd be on the top podium with gold.

With one arm, he clamped my torso to his face. With the other hand, the one that was two fingers deep into my pussy, he began to stroke. Fast. Hard.

Hard and fast. I released his dick on a deep moan, unable to focus with this new intensity in my pussy.

As soon as my mouth was free of him, Owl's mouth clamped down around my clit. His tongue swatted and slurped at me from every direction. So fast it made my head spin. His fingers continued to work, never ceasing their hard and fast motion on my G-spot.

"Come for me, Kira."

I came. Fast and hard. The pleasure radiating out of me in every direction. My hips jerked, but Owl held me clamped down to him. He didn't stop his tongue swiping or his finger jerking during or after my orgasm.

In fact, there was no after the orgasm. It kept going and going.

Somewhere outside an animal cried out for help. Its groans alternated between high-pitched pleas and deep grunts of indulgence. But I knew that was no animal. I knew it was me. I couldn't spare the care or attention to be ashamed at the sounds I made, or worried if others might hear me. I was too far-gone.

Owl didn't stop the motions of his tongue or his fingers until my body collapsed down onto his in exhaustion. And even then, he didn't let me go. He licked at me, slowly and carefully, like someone would lick up the crumbs of a superb dessert.

He made sure to avoid my clit as he slopped up the drippings of the orgasm that lasted longer than I knew was possible. I held still while he did, unable to stop him even if I wanted to. My head rested against something hard and warm and throbbing. It was his dick. I sighed as I looked at it. I was too limp to do anything about its firmness.

NINE

Sometime later, Owl rolled me over and pulled me onto his chest. I lay on him; me naked and drenched in sweat and my own cum, him fully clothed, calm, cool, and collected. He'd even put his barely touched, still hard dick back into his pants.

He pet me on my head, running his fingers through my hair. "Good girl."

I closed my eyes against the sensations rumbling through me at the sound of those two words. "I told you, don't call me your girl. It messes with my head, especially after an orgasm like that. Unless you want me running around calling you my boyfriend."

I hoped that sounded light-hearted and not as real as I wished it to be. We were just fucking. That was all. That was enough. This wasn't a relationship.

I didn't need a boyfriend and all that status entailed; all the anxieties about where he was and who he was with.

Owl's phone sat on my dresser next to the vibrator he'd given me. I looked away from the phone though my fingers itched to crack his code and hack into his social profiles. I turned my face into his chest, into that space that seemed to cradle the shape of my head perfectly. Owl was giving me exactly what I needed right now. I didn't need to screw this up with my special brand of crazy.

"I want them," he said.

"You want what?"

"Your orgasms."

I rose from my comfortable spot and peered down at him. His dark eyes were intense as they peered back at me. "You just gave me what will likely be the biggest orgasm of my entire life. Probably the biggest orgasm of a lot of women's lives."

Owl stared back at me. There was something in his gaze that should have unsettled me, something dark and indefinable. Instead of backing away with caution, I poked it with a stick.

"Explain what you mean," I said.

"You come for no one but me. Do you understand, Shakira?"

I tried to make sense of his words. I already didn't come for anyone but him. He was my tour guide into the Land of Orgasm and I didn't see anyone else around for miles. "You mean you want to be the only guy in my bed?"

"You can fuck other guys if you want," he clarified. "But you will not come for them. You will not have an orgasm while they are inside of you or while they're touching you. Only with me."

Yeah, I really didn't understand how that was different from the status quo? "Do you get to fuck other women and come for them?"

Owl thought on that for a second. "I won't come for anyone but you."

The concession shocked me. But it wasn't enough. "If I agree to this, to only come for you, I don't want you to make anyone else come either."

He frowned as though it were an absurd condition. Instead of saying no outright, he pursed his lips and thought it over.

My heartbeat so hard in my chest I thought it was trying to punch me from the inside out for ruining the good thing my vagina had going on. I was ready to concede, to agree to let him fuck other women so long as he kept coming back and making me come every night.

But then he said, "Deal." He gave me a peck on the cheek and then stood and straightened his clothes. He tucked in his shirt and zipped up his pants.

"What do you mean deal?" I said.

"I won't make any other woman come but you. I won't come for anyone but you. In exchange, your orgasms belong to me. You don't come for anyone else, and that includes by your own hand."

I felt more rattled at this change of events than when he stuck his tongue up my ass.

"Now, you're my girl," he winked at me with a smile.

My heart leaped at the words. My heart grew hands and grabbed the statement with everything in it. "I told you, when you say things like that, it messes with my head."

Owl shrugged. "They're just words; my girl, my man. You can have them if you want them."

"What are you saying, Owl? You need to be real clear with me right now."

He shrugged again, not quite meeting my eyes. "I have what I want from you; your orgasms. You can have those words if they're that important to you. You can call me your boyfriend."

He picked up the vibrator from my nightstand.

"Remember to use this on yourself tonight. Set it to medium this time, seven minutes now. You are not allowed to come while you use it. If you come, I'll know."

Owl set the vibe back on the dresser. He leaned down and kissed my forehead. Then he bent down and kissed my lips. "I'll be back tomorrow night. Don't forget to work out my pussy. I want it throbbing by the time I come back to visit it."

He was out the door before my mind could form a coherent thought. What the hell had I agreed to?

TEN

"Ellie, wait up."

After looking down at my watch, I realized that there was no way I'd make the bus across town. I'd spent a little extra time with the vibe exercises Owl had prescribed for me this evening.

For the past few days the vibe was the first thing I reached for when I woke up. In a way, it was like reaching for Owl, who never stayed over. He'd let me rest on his chest in that space between his pecs that seemed as though it was made for the shape of my head. But as soon as I dozed off, he'd be up and out of the door.

Tonight, I was meeting him for one of his street races. I'd hoped that afterwards we'd go to his place and I might weasel my way between his sheets until morning. But I was late for the bus after spending an extra minute with the vibe.

I'd come so close to coming on my own, which I knew I wasn't supposed to do. It didn't matter anyway because I couldn't get myself over that cliff that led to oblivion. Not without him. I'd lain in my bed, frustrated for thirty minutes as the throbbing in my clit subsided.

I was coming to regret the deal I'd made with him that I'd only come with him. I hadn't believed that my body would only respond to him, and not to me. I was wrong.

So, now I was running across the school parking lot in a tiny mini skirt and fuck me heels watching the city bus's exhaust in the distance. "Ellie, do you think you could give me a ride, sis?"

Ellie, who stood in her knee length skirt and flat shoes, hesitated as she looked me over. I understood her hesitancy. She'd only known me for a few weeks. And right now I looked anything but the over-achieving, Dean's List scholar that I was.

Watching the war rage on Ellie's face between what she knew about me and what she'd likely been raised to believe about girls that dressed like me, I assumed there was also a touch of racial prejudice going on. She probably assumed I was headed to the hood because I was black.

"Sure," she said sounding anything but certain of her decision.

We made our way over to her car. Her patent leather shoes tapped the ground quietly as though to not disturb the asphalt below it. My stilettoed boots struck the pavement with an attitude that would've woke up the worms burrowed in the warm earth.

"Wow," I said as Ellie unlocked the doors of her car with a key fob. "This is your ride, sis?"

She nodded, her chest rising with pride inside her cardigan.

"I guess it fits your personality. I mean, I get it, sis." I strapped on the seat belt. "You're studying to be an entomologist and you have a lady bug car."

I gave her directions, and we headed away from the trendy market district where most of the college students did their shopping and entertainment. We drove past the docks where many of the underclass, who didn't work, coalesced. We pulled up into a seedy part of town.

"It's just over here." I pointed to a one-way street with no houses. Lined up in the parking lot of an abandoned factory were rows upon rows of sleek cars.

"Where's your house?" Ellie said.

"Girl, I don't live in this jacked neighborhood. I'm just meeting this guy here."

"Is he your boyfriend?"

Even though Owl said I could call him my boyfriend, I didn't. Not until he called me his girlfriend. I'd learned that lesson with Sergio. "He's not boyfriend material, sis. Just someone I'm hooking up with."

Wow, I sounded convincing to myself. Ellie nodded as though she understood, but I caught the wince in her eye. She was obviously a virgin. I doubted she believed in sex before marriage. My guess was that she was one of those girls who wouldn't even kiss a guy until he'd met her parents and gave her a promise ring. And when she got married, they'd likely have sex once a week with the lights off. It'd be quick, painless, and joyless. Poor thing.

I did a quick application of lip-gloss and rearranged the girls in my top for an additional advantage. "Thanks for the ride, sis."

"So, is this someone's birthday party?" Ellie asked.

"It's a street race."

Owl had explained he and his friends did street

races every weekend. They moved the races each week to avoid the cops, but they had no trouble. A good number of the cops looked the other way while placing bets on his crew.

"I'll see you on Monday, sis."

I left Ellie behind and made my way into the melee. It wasn't hard to spot Owl and his friends. They were the ones surrounded by all the women. I recognized them from my first night with Owl in the club's parking lot after dumping Sergio and having my first real fuck.

There was the white guy that looked like he'd been carved by Michelangelo. He was blond with a jaw that had to have been sculpted from stone. He had his hand up a woman's shirt while he was talking to the black guy with the bald head and dark eyes that were so intense I felt their burn from feet away. The brutha's attention was on the Michelangelo while a girl rode his hip.

Both men looked up at my approach. Each man broke out licentious grins as they scanned my body. My steps faltered under their gazes. I stopped walking all together when I saw Owl.

Owl leaned against a black Charger while a girl arched her breasts into him. His eyes were on her breasts, but his hands were tucked under his armpits.

I hesitated. I had to remind myself that he wasn't my boyfriend, not for real. Not until he said the words. He wasn't cheating. He was sticking to his word. He said he was only fucking me. He was only looking at her. That was allowed. He was clearly keeping his hands off her. I should be thrilled.

But then the girl reached out her hand to his chest. He stared down at her hand and then back at her. The look in his eyes said back off, but in a playful way. His eyes were not forceful. I got the feeling that if she'd kept it there he would've let her. He wasn't breaking the rules, she was.

Owl looked up and saw me. "There's my girl." He came forward, brushing off the girl's touch without a second glance. "Come meet my boys, Kira."

He took my hand in his own. It took my feet an extra second to uproot from the spot I'd been standing and staring in. I let go of the stake I'd had on that spot and allowed Owl to lay claim to my entire body when he wrapped an arm around my waist.

"This is Eagle and Crow." Owl pointed to the black and blond one.

The two hadn't broken their gazes off my body the whole time. The black one winked. The blond one tugged on his upper lip as he stared openly at my breasts.

"And this is Hawk."

If I'd thought the other guys were big, Hawk nearly blocked out the moon. He stood far over six feet with an upper body the size of a truck. There was an air of authority surrounding him. He was the only one who didn't leer at me.

"Hi," I said.

Hawk spared me a brief glance. "Who's your friend?"

I followed the direction of his gaze. Ellie still sat in her parked Beetle under a streetlight. "She's just my ride here."

Hawk's lips spread in a predator's smile. His eyes narrowed on his prey. "Invite her over."

I knew Ellie was smart enough to stay away from a man like this. No way could she handle him if I could barely handle my little tryst with Owl. I wasn't about to invite a lamb into the lion's den. "She said she was meeting her boyfriend after dropping me off."

Hawk turned his gaze back to me. I knew those dark eyes saw straight through my lie.

"Hey, Owl," a girl in short shorts sauntered up and insinuated herself between us. "I came to give you your good luck kiss." The girl turned her face southward and ran her hands over the crotch of Owl's jeans.

"Thank you Pepper, but I'm good." Owl moved out of her reach and slung his arm around me.

Pepper raised an eyebrow at me, then shrugged and went on to Eagle. "Hey E, I brought these for you." She handed Eagle a thong. He put them in his back pocket. "Crow, you wanna suck 'em for good luck?" She lifted her shirt and put one of her pink nipples into Crow's mouth.

Hawk tore his gaze away from Ellie's still parked car and put his hand in Pepper's shorts as Crow sucked her tits. I tried not to gape. I'd seen scenes like this in pornos. But I couldn't help it.

Pepper gave herself over to the men completely, closing her eyes and letting lose a deep sigh. The three guys descended on her like vultures. They surrounded her, taking parts of her body into their own. It was like they were eating her alive, but it looked like a good death. A really, really good death.

Owl stepped in front of the scene, blocking my view.

"So, when you said you were watching two girls fucking the other day, I'm guessing your boys were around."

"Yeah," he said. He took my hand and tucked it into the crook of his elbow, leading me away.

"So you guys…"

"Like to share pussy and watch?" Owl finished for me. "Yeah."

"That's a healthy lifestyle."

"Says the woman who insisted on fucking one lame ass man at a time."

Owl's tone held no sting. Since I'd met him, I'd never once heard him raise his voice or lash out in anger.

"Maybe you should try things my way." He leaned down and licked the tip of my ear. "It's been working out for you so far."

A shiver went down my spine at the light contact. I looked back at Pepper who had a huge grin on her face as the men steadied her on her feet and sent her away.

Owl deposited me on the sidelines. "See you at the finished line." He turned to walk towards his car.

"Hey," I called after him.

He turned back.

"You don't need me to kiss it for good luck?"

Owl grinned. "I don't need luck, baby. Just keep my pussy warm. I'll give it a kiss when I get back." Owl headed back into the melee and got into his car.

THOUGH OWL and his crew won the race, they took awhile to make their way back to the party at the end of the finished line. They all seemed really jacked when they pulled up. Owl hopped out, grabbed me and pushed me up against the back of his car. He pressed his hips into mine and clamped his mouth on my neck. I almost went with it until I heard the roar of the crowd.

"Owl," I shoved at him.

"What?" He looked up at me.

"We have an audience."

He frowned as though I made no sense. And then he sighed and let me go. I nearly reneged at the sight of his annoyance, but public sex performer was not the girl that I was. The backseat of a car was one thing, but on display on the trunk was another.

As though he read my mind, Owl opened the door to his car. "Yo, I'll see ya'll back at the house. I'm gonna take Kira home."

My heart sank. He wasn't taking me back to his place. He was dismissing me. It was over. A hollowness settled between my thighs, in my chest.

Owl got into the driver's seat. He shut the door

and turned in his seat to stare at me, eyes expectant. "Seat belt," he said.

I reached for the strap and pulled it on. He reached down and tightened the strap over my torso. His hands brushed my breasts. I inhaled, my body betraying me. He leaned into my lips. His tongue swept my lower lip, and I opened for him. He pulled away before I could capture his lip.

He reached in the dashboard and pulled out a vibe that was the same make and model as the one he'd given me. "In you," he said.

"Whaa?"

With his right hand he spread my thighs. The perspiration between my legs gave him easy access. He pushed my panties to one side and inserted the vibe. I was already trembling from that much contact.

"I'm turning it up to high."

My eyes flew open. I'd been practicing on medium all week. I could barely handle that much sensation.

He turned the dial up. I grabbed the edges of the seat. My hips tilted up. My heels rose off the ground and I pressed my toes into the floor. Owl chuckled and floored the gas.

I couldn't lurch forward, I couldn't move at all.

The seat belt held me fast. I was certain the restraints coupled with the double vibrations would send me over in no time.

Owl got onto the highway, already breaking the speed limit on the on ramp. The vibe in my pussy and the vibrations of the car were too much. My body needed to release, but instead of going over I teetered on the edge.

Owl pushed the car even faster. The needle on the speedometer shook as it ticked higher and higher on the dial. My body wanted to lurch over the edge, out the door, through the windshield. Anything to break through this last barrier to the relief I craved.

Finally, Owl pulled over onto the side of the highway. Cars whizzed past us. We parked underneath a street lamp.

Owl undid his seat belt. He leaned over into my seat. He pulled my tight seatbelt until it was even tighter across my torso. I couldn't move. He pushed my panties further to the side, until they were in the crease of my thighs, and thrust his fingers inside me. It moved the vibe deeper into me. He curled his fingers into my G-spot and rubbed my clit with his thumb.

"Owl, please." I panted. Tears pooled in my eyes.

He studied my face. "You know, Kira, when you're ready to come your eyes crinkle. It's like your going to cry, but you don't. Your mouth makes the perfect shape of a heart. It's beautiful." He kissed the edges of my lips as he stroked me with his fingers.

"I want to come, Owl. I want it so bad, but I can't. I can't."

"Tell me who it belongs to, Kira."

"It's yours, Owl."

"What's mine?"

"My pussy. My orgasms. Please..."

"Give it to me, baby. Give me what's mine. Come for me, Kira."

And just like that, I came. I would've doubled over with the force of the orgasm if the seatbelt wasn't restraining me.

"Don't stop, Kira."

He pulled the vibe out and put it on my clit. I kept contracting. My legs shook, bouncing up and down on my toes.

"Don't stop, baby."

My chest heaved, my fingernails cracked, my head arched back beyond the headrest. My entire body shook under his command. I came and came until he told me I could stop.

I think I may have passed out because when I

opened my eyes again we were at my dorm. Owl walked me up the stairs, slowly and carefully on my weak knees. Once inside my room, he undressed me and tucked me into the bed.

As he pressed the sheets under my shoulders, my eyes were on level with his crotch. "You don't need me to...?"

He looked down at the line of my vision. "No baby, I'm good," he grinned.

"You haven't fuck-me fucked me, been inside of me, in days. Don't you need to, you know?"

"No," he kissed me on my forehead. "I'm good." He reached over and turned out my lamp.

"So... you're gonna go and..."

"Stick my dick in some other pussy?" He leaned against the wall. His features were plunged in darkness so I couldn't read his expression, but I knew he was grinning at me. "I told you I wouldn't fuck anybody but you when you gave me control of your orgasms. I'm a man of my word, Kira."

Owl moved to the door. The light from the hallway cast him in a garish silhouette. "Sleep well, baby."

My body did exactly what he told me to. Before he shut the door, I was out like the light.

ELEVEN

"No. I didn't fuck Owl."

I looked Ellie up and down as she denied fucking my boyfriend -no. Not, my boyfriend. My lover? My fuck buddy?

I didn't even know what the hell we were. I knew that he'd promised he wouldn't be with another girl so long as I only came for him. But Ellie had the look of a girl who'd come recently. I knew that look because I'd been doing a lot of it these past couple of weeks.

Ellie stood on the curb waiting for a ride to Owl and his boys' party alongside me. She'd lost that innocent sheen since the last time I'd seen her. Presently, she looked like she'd been thoroughly fucked and was eager for more. If she was out here waiting for a ride, I had to assume that Hawk got his hands on her, likely more than just his hands. I was relieved to hear that Owl didn't have a hand in whatever went on between Ellie and the Watchers Crew; that Owl had kept his word just like he'd told me he would.

"But he was there," Ellie said. "He watched."

I stiffened. I tried to keep my face passive, but inside my head my thoughts were paddling furiously, like a duck in still waters.

The deal Owl and I struck had been that he wouldn't fuck another girl. We'd said nothing about him watching another girl get fucked.

He hadn't touched her. He said he liked to watch. He hadn't lied. He hadn't cheated. But still, I felt a sense of betrayal.

"I don't know you, Ellie," I said. "But you look like you don't have much experience with the world. So I'll do you a favor and tell you this much: a woman shouldn't have to share her man. If she shares him with another, then he never was hers to begin with."

I cringed at the sound of my mother's voice coming out of my mouth. The sound of an engine growling halted any further conversation between Ellie and I. Owl pulled up in his car. The growling engine gave the illusion that the dragons on either side of his vehicle were the ones puffing out hot flames from the exhaust.

Owl hopped out of the driver's side with his normal cocky grin plastered over his face. He didn't glance over at Ellie. He came straight for me.

"Hey, baby," he said.

All I could think of was those dark, intense eyes watching Ellie as she came. Why hadn't he come over and watched me come instead? What did she have that I didn't? It had to be that whole innocent thing. I couldn't compete with that. My innocence had been given away years ago. Suspicion and bitterness were all that was left in its wake.

Owl reached for me, but I jerked away from him. I crossed my arms over my chest and turned my head away.

He frowned, and then he looked over at Ellie. I studied him as he studied her, trying to gage if he lingered on some part of her in particular. Was it the way she dressed? Her breasts? The demure look in her eyes? I could probably mimic that.

But Owl's glance was swift. He didn't linger on

any of Ellie's body parts. He looked her dead in the eye. "Hey, Ellie. Hawk said you needed a ride."

He opened the rear passenger door of his car and Ellie climbed in. "Buckle up," he said to her. "It's going to be a bumpy ride."

He shut the door and turned back to me. He leaned against the frame of the car, crossed his arms over his chest, and raised that eyebrow. His body was at ease while mine was coiled with tension.

His eyes took a slow path from my heels, up my legs. He smiled when he came to my crotch area. It was a secret smile, a possessive smile. He bit his lip when he got to my breasts. Then those calm, cool eyes reached my face. He said nothing. Just like he'd build me up and wait for me to come, he simply waited for my anger and insecurities to explode.

"Did you fuck her?"

Owl cocked his head, observing me. "Do you think I fucked her?"

Right there, in that moment, I knew he didn't. But suspicion and jealousy were like a disease inside of me. My own reasoning had never been able to manage the symptoms. I reached for the only thing that had ever been able to temporarily relieve the side effects.

"I need you to tell me the truth," I said. "I need you to say it."

In the past, I'd often caught my boyfriends red-handed. I'd seen Sergio with his hands all over that woman in the club the night I'd met Owl. Sergio had said it wasn't what I thought it was. If Owl hadn't have been there, with his hand holding me still, I may have gone back to Sergio because hearing those false words would've rung true in my messed up head.

I didn't want to leave Owl. I needed him to stay and say the words. To deny any wrongdoing.

"I wanted to fuck Ellie," he said.

I shut my eyes. Those were not the words I needed to hear. They made the sickness flare. My palms sweat. Hives broke out on my neck. I knew that if I put my hand to my head I'd feel the signs of a fever coming on.

"But," he said, "I told you I wouldn't."

I opened my eyes. "She said you watched the others fuck her."

"I did. I watched her get fucked." He waited patiently while I swallowed that bitter pill. "As much as Ellie likes to get fucked by the crew, she only comes for Hawk. That's good for Hawk because he likes to watch others get his girl off. Did I want to participate? Hell, yeah. Ellie comes off shy, but once you get your hands on her, she doesn't hold back."

I looked back into the car seeing red in the reflection of the tinted windows. The tint blocked my view of eager, easy Ellie who sat comfortably out of the day's heat while I was a blazing cauldron of jealousy.

When I spoke, it was with my mother's voice again. "A woman shouldn't have to share her man. If she shares him with another, then he never was hers to begin with."

Owl took my chin in his fingers gently, but his control over my head was absolute. "That is complete bullshit. Whoever told you that was selfish, self-centered, and had low self-esteem." He held my chin firm. He wouldn't let me look away from him.

"My mother told me that."

"Then I'm sorry about your daddy issues."

I jerked away from him. He let me go this time. "You don't know anything about me."

"More bullshit," he said calmly. "I know what's important to you because I listen to you. I pay attention to your needs and I respect them. I did not fuck Ellie." He enunciated every word. "I didn't put my dick into her. I didn't lick her pussy. I didn't kiss her.

These are the things that are important to you fuck-wise, right?"

I didn't respond. I didn't need to. We both knew he was right.

"It's selfish of you to ask me to give up the things I enjoy so you can pretend that you're more comfortable with what we have between us. When, at the end of the day, you're not. The reason your relationships end, Kira, is not because the men you choose cheat. It's because you don't trust them to begin with."

I turned away from him, but he rounded on me.

"There is something between us," he said. "I feel it too, baby."

I looked up at him. My hands had been crossed over my chest. I now clasped my hands together at my heart.

"But just because I feel something different, something more, for you," he continued, "that doesn't mean I don't want to fuck other girls."

My fingers fell away from each other. My hands fell away from my heart and down to my sides.

"But I won't." Owl reached for me. "Not until you trust me, and you're comfortable with the idea."

I watched the words come out of his mouth. "I don't understand you."

"I don't understand your need to keep tabs on my dick when it's not in you. I gave you my word when you gave me control of your orgasms. Do you think I'm going to change my mind, change how I feel, because I dip into some random pussy?"

"Most men think with their dicks."

"Dicks aren't the dumb instruments women think they are. You just encountered a bunch of assholes. I don't mind if you fuck another dude, Kira. As long as they know how to treat you right. I want you to feel good even when I'm not around."

"You want me to fuck your friends? Like Ellie?"

Owl shrugged. "You might like it."

"But I thought you didn't want me to come for anybody but you."

He smiled. "I don't. And you won't. Because that," he pointed to my pussy, "is all mine."

That one word sailed into my brain and stirred up all kinds of emotions.

Mine.

"How's that not you being selfish?" I challenged him. "Keeping my orgasms all to yourself."

"Because I'm willing to share them with others. I just need to be the one in control of them."

That made no kind of sense. Before I could launch into an argument, Owl brought me to him with a light kiss on the lips. His tongue did a slow invasion of my mouth. His hand slipped down to my ass. His fingers roamed into my crack and reached around.

"Tell me it's mine, Kira."

There was no hesitation in my body to give over to him. Owl might profess to not think with his dick, but I was clearly thinking with my clit with his hands all over me. "It's yours, Owl."

More than anything, I wanted to be his. I wanted to be wrapped up in the security of belonging to someone. I wanted to feel safe that I wouldn't be left alone.

None of my other boyfriends had claimed me like this. Owl openly called me his. Most of my exes didn't like PDA because they were always on the hunt for the next girl. But Owl put his arm around me out in public, in the middle of his friends, and in front of girls he clearly had been fucking on a regular basis. Here we were in the middle of the school parking lot, making out for all to see that we were together in this... whatever the hell it was.

"Tell me I'm the only one who presses that button, Kira."

I felt my clit pulse in response to his voice as

though it was his pet and he'd called its name. It sat up on its hind legs, throbbing for a treat.

"Tell me I'm the only one that can make you shake, make you beg for release."

My knees felt weak just at the mention of what he'd done to me in the past, what he could do to me. My clit was mewling, salivating. All it would take was one flick of his finger and I'd purr in release.

I tried to pull away, to catch my breath, and then I saw. We had an audience. Most of the faces I didn't recognize, but a few I did. The men looked on with appreciation. The women's faces were a mix of envy and judgment.

"Owl, stop. Not here."

Owl only had eyes for me. He ignored the crowd, but he did pull back. He didn't look pleased to have been told to stop.

My clit whimpered under the glare of his stare. His fingers pressed into my hip. If he lowered them just another inch, I would start to tremble out in the middle of the street, with all these people watching. I felt helpless, completely at his mercy.

"Owl please. Don't."

And then, finally, he broke out into a smile. "I love it when you beg, baby." He pecked me on the cheek and then opened the front passenger door for me.

I got in, shaken by how close I'd come to coming.

I'd completely forgotten Ellie was in the backseat.

TWELVE

Inside the house it looked like something out of a rap video. Pulsing music blared from speakers set in the four corners of the room. Porn played on the flat screen mounted on the wall. The scene on display mirrored the scene in reality; an orgy.

There were near naked and fully naked girls prancing around the room, huddled in corners, or splayed across furniture. Some appeared to wait patiently in a queue like they would for a ride at an amusement park, only the ride was a guy's dick. Other girls took to the floor or up against a wall and rode each other.

No act looked sacred, and no one appeared exclusive. I watched one girl slide off one guy's dick and back her ass onto another guy's cock.

I watched a guy pull his dick out of the ass of one girl and put it into the mouth of another. Neither woman protested. In fact, the girl who'd just had her ass fucked curled up next to them and watched the guy fuck the other girl's face with hungry eyes. Not an ounce of jealousy or bitterness crinkled her sated face.

And then there was Ellie.

Ellie made a beeline to Hawk who sat in a chair that reminded me of a throne. There had been another girl on his lap, but he shooed her away to make room for Little Miss Eager and Easy.

Ellie sat down next to Hawk. His eyes were rapt on her. I knew that look in Hawk's eyes. I'd seen it in the mirror more times than I could count. It was clear to me that Hawk wanted more than a fling with Ellie.

Ellie stood and got undressed in front of the room full of people. Her eager fingers shook as she removed each article of clothing, but she stayed focused on Hawk as though his was the only attention that mattered to her. Once she was naked, Hawk turned her around, so she faced outward, for every one to see. He slipped his thick dick into her and began to fuck her.

I knew I should look away, which was an odd thought. I'd had no problems staring at everyone else in the room as they performed sexual acts I'd never seen in any online porno. I hadn't looked away from any of them. But it was different when it was someone I knew.

I knew Ellie. Not well, but well enough to realize I'd be looking her in the eye tomorrow. When I saw her tomorrow, dressed in her skirt and those patent leather shoes, this is what I would remember. Her pink-tipped breasts bouncing up and down on her chest. Her bare pussy being spread wide, dripping its juices down a dark dick. Her pale face contorted in unabashed ecstasy as her body shook and she came hard.

I was breathing just as hard as Ellie when Hawk embraced her. He turned her head around and looked at her like she was a prize. If I'd felt like a voyeur before, I was a down right Peeping Tom now. That look was by far the most intimate thing going on in this room full of naked cunts and cocks. But just as soon as I'd seen it, it was gone. Hawk shuttered his expression and handed Ellie over to Eagle.

I let out a strangled breath as I watched the exchange. I couldn't understand it? Hawk clearly had feelings for Ellie, and she obviously carried the same torch for him. But he'd just let his woman go off with another man, and she didn't seem the least bit put out about it. There was a spark of excitement in her eyes as Eagle carried her off.

Owl came up behind me. He didn't touch me. He didn't speak. He rested his head against mine. I felt his breath on my ear as Eagle put a vibrator inside Ellie.

My own core ached to be filled with the vibe Owl had given me to practice with. I'd only used it twice today; when I woke up and just after lunch. I'd assumed we'd be playing together tonight in his bed. I was getting the idea that the scene before me was my orgasmic preparation for the rest of the night.

Owl's arms came around me. He wrapped me up in a tight hug and then rested his hands on my waist. He didn't push himself into me from behind. That was me. I rested my ass against his erection, seeking some source of relief from the constant pitter-patter of my eager pussy.

We stayed like that; quietly wrapped up in each other as we watched Ellie come and come some more at the hands of Eagle and his vibe. Then Crow and his tongue. Then Crow and Eagle, forming a human centipede, with one dick in Ellie's pussy and another in her mouth.

All this while Hawk sat by and watched. His expression was one of pure delight and joy as he watched his girl get worked over until she was near to passing out from all the pleasure. Ellie's eyes were glued on Hawk as she sucked and fucked his friends. The two couldn't stop staring at each other. And they all did it out in the open. No closed doors. No lying or hiding.

When Crow and Eagle were done with Ellie, they handed her back to Hawk who curled her up in his lap and stroked her hair. With Ellie's eyes closed he didn't bother to mask his adoration of her.

"Hey Owl, you wanna fuck?" A naked brunette made her way over to us.

"No, thank you," he said. "My girlfriend's here with me."

The entire room went out of focus for me. He'd told me that it was fine if I wanted to call him my boyfriend. This was the first time he'd claimed me as his girlfriend. Hearing that one word, my pussy throbbed so hard I thought I was about to come right there.

"Does she wanna fuck?" The brunette eyed me.

"No, I'm going to take care of her." Owl used

that tone of voice again. The soft steel that appeared pliable. "Don't I, Kira? Don't I always take care of you?"

His words, his voice, they each wrapped around me tighter than his arms ever could. But looking up, looking around the room at all the faces staring back at us, watching me, I struggled against his hold on me.

"Isn't this what you wanted, Shakira? For every one to know that we're together, that I'm your man, and you're my girl?"

God, he did know me. He had been paying attention. He was giving me exactly what I wanted, but in a way I'd never expected to receive it. He'd turned down a sexual request right in front of me. He'd staked his claim out in the open, in front of all his friends. He'd called me his girlfriend. He'd said I was his man.

He brought me back into his arms and turned me to face Eagle and Crow working over another girl. She was laid stretched out on the couch, her head arched over the armrest. Crow kneeled on the armrest plunging his dick into her mouth while tweaking her nipples.

"You see Crow's fingers on her breasts, baby?

See him making those tight little circles like you like? Imagine how hard her nipples are."

Owl's hands were nowhere near my breasts but my nipples tightened into little points instantly. I ached for relief. I arched my chest up, but he didn't move his hands.

Instead he used his hands to turn my hips a little to the right. The girl's body was stretched out on the couch and between her thighs I saw the cord of a vibe snaking out. Her body pulsed in time to Eagle thrusting into her ass.

"She's got the same vibe you use. Can you see her pussy quivering from here? Think about how your toy feels inside of you. Think about me turning up the dial to high."

Everyone in the room faded except for Eagle, Crow, and the sound of Owl's voice in my ear. I no longer saw the girl lying between the two men. It was now me on that couch getting worked over by two other men while Owl whispered in my ear.

Crow tilted *my* head back as he plunged his dick all the way down *my* throat until *I* gurgled. Eagle rimmed *my* ass with the thick head of his cock. It was *my* body that was trembling and shaking from both ends.

"Are you cheating if you enjoy watching them?

Does it make you want to fuck me any less? Or does it make you want to fuck me more?"

More. It made me want Owl more. I stopped struggling and squirmed in an altogether different way.

"I could watch you get fucked like that, baby. Watch you get high just like Eagle and Crow made Ellie high, just like they're making that girl high. As long as you remember who it belongs to. That pussy doesn't come without my say so."

Just Owl saying the word *come* had me whimpering. The thought of his friends surrounding me like that, giving their undivided attention to my pleasure, suddenly I couldn't remember what my objections were.

"But you said I couldn't come with another man," I protested. "You want your boys to fuck me without satisfying me?"

"You used to fuck all the time without coming, Kira. Shit like that doesn't go down here. A woman always leaves satisfied. I want to show you that you can have a satisfying fuck without coming."

I had no interest in fucking without coming. I was about to tell him so when something caught the corner of my eye. The woman who'd offered to fuck Owl a moment ago, she still stood near us. Her hand was in her pussy as she leaned against the wall. Her eyes were locked on Owl's mouth, listening to him speak to me. I saw her chest rise and fall rapidly as she approached her orgasm all because of his voice.

I stopped squirming in the good way. The thought of Owl with another woman sent a cold sliver of water down my spine and between my legs. Owl noticed my stiffness and let me go. I turned to face him.

"Did you bring me here to butter me up?" I asked. "So I'd get with the program of you fucking other girls?"

Owl tilted his head to the side and sighed. I felt like I was on a high stakes game show and I'd just gotten the million dollar question wrong.

"I brought you here to share with you something I enjoy," he said. "I wanted you to learn more about me and my needs tonight."

I looked around the room at the fucking orgy that was in full swing. I watched the strangers open themselves up to whoever was available and then move on after they were done. "Owl, I don't think I can do this."

"I haven't asked you to do anything but come for me and only me." He reached out his hand. "Come on, let's go."

I clenched my fingers into a fist and dug my heels into the hardwood floors.

"I'm not going to force you to do anything you don't want to do, Kira. Just let me show you."

"Where are we going?"

"To my bedroom."

THIRTEEN

Owl led me back through the kitchen, and down the steps into the basement. There were only a few steps on the stairs. From the top of the stairs I saw a spacious room. There was a black dresser, which looked as though it could be in a show room. It was spotless and orderly with every toiletry lined up by width and height. Every item of jewelry was arranged by precious metal. In another corner was a workout area where the weights were all lined up according to size. The bed was not only made, the corners were up to military par.

"Sit down on the bed," Owl commanded.

I came down the stairs and made my way over to his bed. In the only window of the room sat plants. Not leafy plants. They were small trees. Bonsai trees

I guessed. Owl's small tools for the miniature trees were in the same perfect alignment as was each branch and leaf of the trees.

Owl bent down and took off my shoes. He held one of my heels in his hands and then massaged the ball and center of my foot. "Relax."

I'd been holding myself up by my elbows. When Owl's thumbs kneaded the ball of my foot, I collapsed back onto the bed. My head rolled to the side as he concentrated his fingers between each of my toes. I could still hear the sounds of music and pleasure from the open door that led up stairs.

"You left the door open."

Owl switched his attention to my other foot, ignoring my comment. "You keep expecting me to leave you, to lie to you, to betray you. I have no intention of doing any of those things, Shakira." His fingers worked at pushing that statement into my thick skull starting from the bottoms of my feet. "Would you like to know why I won't?"

He didn't wait for my answer. He rose and went to the top drawer of his dresser. When he turned back around he had a length of rope in his hands.

"What are you planning to do with that?" I said.

He smirked. "What do you think?"

"Owl, you know my people have issues with rope and bonds."

He let out a laugh. "That's only because they weren't tied up by one of my people." He reached for my hands, his eyes asking for permission.

I looked from him to the ropes and then back again. "So bondage is your kink?"

"Control is my kink. Control of your pleasure. Controlling your orgasm. Controlling the intensity."

"Of course," I said with another glance around his orderly room. "You're a control freak."

"I'm no different than you and your can of pens," he grinned. "Monogamy is a fetish. You deny yourself contact with other partners. You only allow them to release with you. How's your need for control different from mine?"

"Mine is more socially acceptable."

Owl smirked. "Yeah, but society lies about being faithful and then they have to hide their needs, and their shame at going out and fulfilling those needs. I'm not hiding anything from you. I've told you what I want, what I need."

I looked again at the rope in his hands. When I handed him my wrists his smirk turned serious. He took my hands in his.

"This is why I'm not going anywhere, Kira. I'm

not going anywhere as long as we're honest about what we need and we're fulfilling each other's needs." He ran the silk over my wrists and looped the ends into a knot. "I'm not playing a game with you. In games somebody has to lose. We do this together and we both get to win."

He pulled the knot tight. The threads of the rope licked at the soft spot on the underside of my wrists.

"You want to feel secure?" He latched the end of the rope to the headboard of the bed, stretching my arms over my head. "I'll give you security, baby. You want my undivided attention?" He chuckled softly as he ran his hand over my neck sending shivers down my spine. "You might come to regret that in a few hours."

I heard a creak from above. Someone was standing on the top of the stairs. They were in the shadows and I couldn't see their faces.

"They don't matter," said Owl. "They're the game. You and me, we're what's real here."

Despite Owl's words, my eyes clung to the shadow on the stairs.

"Eyes on me." He used that tone of soft steel.

My eyes immediately found his. My hands were tied to the bed. My legs spread wide, but my skirt covered me. Owl sat down on the bed to obstruct the view of the onlookers.

"I'll untie you if you tell me to," he said in his quiet, soothing voice as his fingers played with the elastic of my panties. "I don't do that safe word bullshit. No, means no. But understand, that if I untie you, I will not be fucking you tonight."

"What?" The shadow on the stairs became hazy to my focused eyes.

"And you will not be allowed to come or play with yourself later when you get home."

"But I can't come without you inside me, or touching me, or talking to me."

The smile that spread across Owl's face was a mix of cruelty and possessiveness. It's what I imagined the devil would look like if he'd trapped an angel and was about to torture her.

Owl yanked the elastic band of my panties. The material fell away and his fingers were inside me, all in one quick motion. "Tell me who it belongs to, Kira."

He curled his fingers upward and hit that spot that made my toes curl. My world shrunk down to his two fingers. Words failed me.

"This is mine, Kira."

He stroked his fingers hard and fast inside me.

I'd been on edge all night, all day. An orgasm instantaneously sprang to the forefront. It pushed back against his fingers, begging to be set free.

But he wouldn't do it. He wouldn't give me the extra pressure I needed. He kept me right on the edge. There was nothing I could do to get the extra bit of friction I needed. With my arms tied over my head, I scratched futilely at the headboard. My heels dug into the mattress, but Owl used his body weight to hold me down.

He took his fingers out. They were soaked with my juices, so much so it dripped down the sides. Owl put his fingers in his mouth. He closed his eyes and suckled.

"Owl, please," I was in tears.

"This pussy, every drop that comes out of it, all belongs to me. Isn't that right, baby." It wasn't a question. He stated a fact and dared me to deny it.

"Please," I whimpered. "I want to come. I need to come."

"Not yet, baby. Let it build."

Let it build? The pressure was stacked up against my hair follicles.

"Fucking bastard." The voice came from the door. "Let the girl come."

The dark shadows that had been in the doorway, the ones I'd been so concerned about moments ago, came down the stairs. My fogged brain recognized Crow and Eagle. Crow had a bath towel wrapped around his waist. Eagle had on a pair of low-slung jeans, unbuttoned. His happy trail grinned back at me above the line of his waistband.

"Want me to suck your breasts, Shakira?" Crow leaned over me. "I can make you come."

I was delirious enough to consider it.

"I'd love to eat that pretty pussy out. Been a minute since I had some prime, dark chocolate." Eagle winked at me.

"No, we're good," said Owl. "We're exclusive. Isn't that right, Kira?"

The three of them joked back and forth about that word and its meaning; exclusive. I heard none of it. Owl's thumb brushed my clit back and forth, light as a feather. Tremors broke out over my body, small quakes that would register low or not at all on a Richter scale.

"If he don't treat you right, you come find us."

"I don't hold back on a girl."

I couldn't tell which of them were speaking. They were a dark, blond blur as the tremors radiated outward. My toes twitched, my palms itched, and butterflies flung themselves inside my belly in a vain attempt to escape.

"She's not going anywhere, are you baby? Kira's my girl. She only comes for me. You wanna show them, baby? You wanna show them how beautiful your orgasms are?"

I was so wound up I didn't care who might see. My body clenched so hard. Everything balled up; my toes, my fingers, my eyes closed.

But I didn't release. I couldn't. Not without his say so. He would say the words soon. I struggled to focus so I wouldn't miss it when the words left Owl's mouth.

"You want it, Kira? You gotta ask for it."

"Puh-puh please..."

"Tell them who it belongs to."

"Yours... It's... Owl."

"That's my girl. Come for me, baby."

Owl was barely touching my clit, just the lightest of swipes. It was enough. The fault line ruptured, splitting a path open from my head to my toes.

My torso arched off the bed as my pussy clenched around an empty channel. I twisted and turned, like a dishtowel that had been soaking all day and now Owl set at ringing every drop of moisture from it. From me.

I came, and I came, and then I came some more. Every time I thought it was over another tremor triggered and quaked through me. When every square inch of my body had been rung dry, I collapsed back onto the bed.

"Fucking hell, Owl."

"Yeah man, that's some fucking voodoo, samurai shit right there."

FOURTEEN

I must have passed out. I opened my eyes when I felt something cold on my head. Owl pressed a cloth to my temple, gently wiping away all the perspiration that had collected there. He looked down at me, but it wasn't with the cocky smile he'd given me on that first night. It wasn't with the smirk he'd given me earlier tonight. It was the same look that Hawk had on his face when Eagle and Crow deposited Ellie back in his lap after they'd put her into a fuck-coma.

There was something about that smile, this smile that pulled at my heartstrings. I tried to stop those ropes from being pulled. Owl didn't believe in relationships and monogamy, not really. This was just temporary. But I couldn't stop the strings of my heart from twisting into a knot. My hands were still tied to his bed.

"Everybody get out," said Owl. "Show's over. I'm gonna fuck my girl now."

I heard the sound of footsteps and then the door being shut. Owl untied my hands and massaged them.

"You okay, baby?"

I had to clear my throat before I could speak. "Yeah. Yeah, I'm okay."

"You satisfied?"

"Now, that I've come, I am."

He grinned at that, his thumb working the kinks out of my wrist. "Will you let me try something?"

My eyes widened. "I don't think I can come again tonight, Owl."

"You might not. But I'd like to come."

I felt like the selfish, self-centered person he'd accused me of being earlier. I hadn't thought about his orgasm since the day we met. In fact I couldn't remember him coming since that day. I sat up and undressed for him.

Once I was naked in his bed, Owl climbed on top of me. He spread my thighs and settled between them. But he didn't enter me. Instead, he kissed me. Slowly, deeply, thoroughly. Then he pulled back and brushed kisses over my eyelids, my nose, my ears.

He scooted down and kissed my breasts. He didn't flick his tongue like he'd normally do to get my clit throbbing with need. His swipes lingered, like a caress. He ran his hands over my back and abdomen, his touch less a tease and more an embrace. He came back up above me, hovering over my lips.

"Owl?"

"Mmm?"

"This doesn't feel like fucking."

I tasted rather than saw the smile on his lips. He wrapped my thighs around his waist and entered me slowly. His rhythm was anything but rushed. His lips never left my mouth or my skin.

We coasted in this cocoon of pleasure for what seemed like hours. Until finally, his movements sped up. His thrusts became frantic. His lips lost their connection with mine. And then, his body stiffened.

Owl opened his eyes, staring down at me, hiding nothing, letting me see every emotion cross over his face. He jerked once, twice, and after the third thrust his face contorted in ecstasy. He groaned deep in his chest. Then he collapsed onto me, into me.

I held onto him. He was the only thing solid in

my life at this moment. My legs were jelly, my heart was putty, and my head was clouded over.

"You satisfied, Kira?"

I hadn't come, but every bone in my body thrummed with joy. I wrapped myself around him and prepared to never let go.

I must've fallen asleep because I dreamed up a life with the two of us. Me working in a firm that allowed flex time for our two children. Owl owned a garage down the street where our kids would go after school. Our son, who had his eyes and my skin coloring, would help his father fix old, antique cars. At night, Owl would tie me up to the bed and fuck me senseless on into the morning.

"Kira?"

When I opened my eyes next, it was to Owl lightly kissing my eyelids. I stretched like a cat and then rolled deeper into his embrace.

"It's time to go home, baby."

I frowned. "Go? Home? Why can't I stay?"

He ran his fingers gently over my brow. "I told you, I don't do sleep overs."

I sat up, the sheets falling away from my bare breasts. "Why not?"

He shrugged. "I always sleep alone. It's nothing personal. I'll come get you tomorrow night. We'll go out on a proper date, like normal people. And then I'll take you back to your place and fuck you into the middle of the night."

"And then you'll leave in the middle of the night?"

"What's the problem?" He took my chin between his fingers and turned me to face him. "You still think I'm going to go out and fuck another girl? I thought we got passed this," he sighed.

"No. No, I believe you." After he'd made love to me, how could I not believe him?

"Then what is it?"

He was right. I had daddy issues. But I didn't want to bring them into this relationship. Because believe it or not, I was starting to think this was the healthiest relationship I'd ever been in in my entire life. And that included my relationship with my parents.

"It's fine," I said. "I can respect your boundaries."

Owl grinned at me, eyes prideful like he was a doctor who'd just witnessed a breakthrough in his patient.

He helped me get dressed and then we went back upstairs. The house was mostly clear of people. A few girls were getting their coats on, preparing to head out the door. Hawk rose from his throne with Ellie in his arms.

"Hey man, I'm about to take Kira home. You want me to take her, too?" Owl indicated the naked Ellie lying happily in Hawk's massive arms.

"No, I got her," said Hawk. "She can sleep it off and drive herself home in the morning."

I caught Ellie's eyes as she went up the stairs in the arms of Hawk, a man who had passed her around to his friends. A man who had been fucking another girl when we came into the house. A man who'd looked at her with the same intensity that the man who called himself my boyfriend had bestowed upon me.

But I was the one walking out the front door while she was being carried upstairs and into a warm bed where she wouldn't have to sleep alone tonight.

"You ready, baby?"

I plastered on a fake smile and took Owl's hand. I followed him out into the cool night air.

FIFTEEN

I sat on the couch in Owl's living room after my morning classes. He'd invited me over for lunch. I'd been hoping for some afternoon delight between the two of us. Owl sat next to me with an arm around my shoulders, his chin rested on the top of my head. The television was off. There was no music. But there was entertainment going on in front of us.

Ellie stood completely naked in the middle of the room. She was sandwiched between Eagle and Crow, who also stood completely bare. Ellie's head rested back against Crow's shoulder as he reached around and played with her taut, pink nipples. Eagle ran his dark hands up and down her body and over her bare pussy.

Crow sat down on the couch before them. He brought Ellie to kneel on the floor. He spread his thighs and offered her his dick. Ellie took it eagerly. Eagle stretched out on the rug beneath her, coming to lay flat on the floor. He guided her hips over his face and pulled her pussy to his lips.

"You hungry, baby?"

It took me a moment to make out Owl's words. I stared at him for a full thirty-seconds as I turned those three words over and over in my head. I was hungry, but it wasn't my stomach that was turning itself in knots, aching to be filled. Owl smiled at me as though he knew exactly what was going on in my body.

He turned away from my mute expression and addressed Hawk who sat in a chair beside us. "You want a sandwich, Hawk?"

"Yeah, thanks man," Hawk said from his chair as he watched his girlfriend get fucked by his two other friends. "Get Ellie some cold orange juice, will you?"

"Sure thing. You want a drink, Kira?"

I swallowed, still unable to get out any words.

Owl smiled. "I'll bring you something." He disappeared into the kitchen, leaving me sitting next to Hawk as his girlfriend climaxed on Eagle's tongue.

I'd watched porn flicks with boyfriends before. I'd sit beside them on the couch trying not to roll my eyes. Or I'd lie next to them in the bed and try not to fall asleep.

Porn was often unrealistic and boring to me. It was done by men for men. The women were only props who stared vacantly at the camera and did a far poorer job than I'd ever done of faking it.

In contrast, I couldn't take my eyes off of the live action scene before me. Crow and Eagle were clearly showing off. They were each vying to see who could make Ellie come harder. I'd never watched another woman come. I'd watched them fake it, of course. But this, the expression on Ellie's face, the sound that came from her gut, this was all real.

I watched Eagle alternately lick long strokes, then fast strokes up and down the length of Ellie's pussy. Then he'd open wide and suck her entire core into his mouth.

Ellie, whose head had been buried in Crow's lap, released Crow's dick with a pop. Eagle grinned triumphantly as Crow scowled.

"I'm gonna come," Ellie announced.

She didn't need to announce it. The signs were clear all over her body. Her hips, which had been moving in a steady wave over Eagle's tongue, jerked erratically. They jerked up and down in quick staccato movements. Her upper body convulsed as her thighs shook. Ellie's eyes closed.

I watched her, trapped in that stillness I'd come to know so well thanks to Owl. It was like riding a roller coaster where you slowed down as you reached the topmost part of the ride. There was a slight pause at the top before you went down. That part where no one is screaming yet. That part where the wind isn't yet on your face. That part where you can feel the space between your heart beats. It's not long. It's just one second, but so much happens in that second to make it feel like an eternity. There's so much awareness in that second that you sense everything.

And then you speed downward. Your heartbeat goes beyond your control. The silence of it fills with your cries. The wind rushes across your body and knocks you over.

I watched Ellie get to that point, that peak. I watched her hold her breath. Her eyes opened. She sought and found Hawk.

Hawk clenched the armrest as he stared at his girlfriend. It was as though he sat right with her on that precipice, experiencing everything she felt in that moment. He held his breath, his chest paused. His fingers were white from clenching the armrest. At the first guttural moan of Ellie's orgasm, Hawk let out a sigh of his own. His body seemed to get knocked back into the chair as hers crashed down into ecstasy.

I realized that he wasn't the only one who'd sighed in relief. My body sagged, too. I sighed right alongside Hawk.

He turned to me and smiled. A prideful look brightened his severe face. He looked like one of those parents whose kid just scored a touchdown at the big game. But instead of scoring the touchdown or playing a flawless concerto, his girlfriend had just came as a result of one man's dick in her mouth and another's tongue in her pussy. I had to ask.

"You're not jealous?"

Hawk frowned, but didn't take his eyes off Ellie as he answered me. "Why would I be jealous?"

I looked back to the scene before us. They'd flipped Ellie around and she was airborne. Crow was still seated on the couch, but he had Ellie's knees in each of his hands. Her legs were thrown behind his shoulders. Her pussy was now in his face. Eagle was standing up. He had Ellie's upper body in his arms. Her face was now impaled on his dick.

"She's fucking other men," I stated the obvious. "I don't understand how you can watch this and not get upset?"

Hawk gave me his attention now. "Look at her. She's happy. She's blissed the fuck out. She's being taken care of."

"By other men."

"Men I trust. Men I know. Men who have my back, so I know they'll have my girl's back. I'm not an asshole. I wouldn't let some random dick fuck my girl."

Ellie moaned around a mouthful of Eagle's dick as she came again, this time on Crow's tongue. Crow smirked at Eagle as he evened the score.

Hawk turned back to the show, sliding his hips down onto the edge of his chair. It reminded me of my dad settling in to watch Sunday football games while my mother made him dinner. But where my father always wore a sour expression and berated my mother's cooking, cleaning, and appearance, Hawk's expression when he looked at Ellie's trembling body was exactly what I had always imagined love would look like.

"And she doesn't mind that you step out on her?" I asked.

"You make me sound like I'm some sleazoid who will fuck anything in a pair of panties."

"Aren't you?"

Hawk smiled, but didn't look away from Ellie who was now upside down. Eagle flipped her hips off Crow and up and over into his face. Ellie's legs went over Eagle's shoulder and her pussy was back under his tongue. With her torso hanging down, Crow took advantage of the situation by teasing one of her breasts with his fingers and another with his tongue.

"I was."

It took me a moment to understand the meaning behind Hawk's two words. I'd lost interest in our conversation watching his girlfriend get flipped and passed around like an acrobatic sex toy.

"Before Ellie, I'd fuck any and everything in a pair of panties. That is if Eagle hadn't gotten them off the girl first. But Ellie..." He shrugged his shoulders as he looked back out at the scene.

Eagle and Crow held Ellie between them now, each taking a hole. They pumped into her pussy and ass like a seesaw until she came for a third time. I had forgotten that I'd asked Hawk a question and he hadn't completed his thought. I'd assumed he wasn't going to continue until he did.

"Ellie settled something in me," he said. "It's like... Do you remember the first time you had an orgasm?"

Did I? It was a very recent memory. I wasn't about to tell Hawk that.

"That's what it's like. Like I'd been jerking off with other girls. It felt good and all. But when Ellie showed up, it was like I actually nutted for the first time in my life. I don't know if that makes any sense?"

It did. It made perfect sense.

"Don't get me wrong, I still like to jerk off. I don't hide that from her. She knows exactly what I'm about. I showed her who I was the first time I touched her, and she accepted it. She accepted me. There are things I like, like rough sex, which I won't do with her. I'll go find somebody else for that. But most of the time I'd rather come home and fuck her, or watch her get fucked. She's fucking beautiful when she comes, isn't she."

I looked over at Ellie. I looked at the unbridled joy on her face. I looked at the two men cradling her in their arms as they brought her to another climax. I looked at the man who loved her revel in her pleasure.

"Most girls try to hold on to their man so tight because they think he'll cheat," Hawk continued. "There's no lies between me and Ellie. No deception, no tricks. No need to hold on because I'm not going anywhere for too long. She knows I'm always coming back home to her, that I'm going to wake up beside her every morning."

Owl returned with a platter of sandwiches and drinks. He planted a kiss on my head before he sat down and we watched Ellie climax for a fifth time.

Crow withdrew from Ellie, his dick dripping with her juices. I watched a few drops splatter down onto the floor. A healthy dollop hung from his cockhead as he made his way over to the side of the couch where I sat. His dick swung between his legs all along the way. The drop of fluid was more sticky than watery and it dangled like a reverse yo-yo with the cum as the string and his cockhead as the roving ball. He reached for a wet wipe, which seemed to be all over the house, and wiped his dick with one wipe and his hands with another.

Eagle hefted a dazed Ellie into his arms. His bare dick also swung back and forth as he made his way across the room. Eagle's dick had been buried up Ellie's ass and there were no drippings coming off of him.

Eagle reached Hawk and handed Ellie over and into her boyfriend's outstretched arms. Hawk curled Ellie up into a fetal position in his lap. He gazed down into her glazed face with that same prideful look of love bright on his face. He stroked her hair and her eyelids and lightly kissed her swollen lips.

My attention broke from their intimate moment when Crow sat down on the other side of me. His dick, which was still semi hard, looked at me from his thigh. He reached over and grabbed one of the sandwiches Owl had made for everyone. "Hey, Kira."

"Hey...hi Crow."

"Want a bite?" He extended the chicken salad sandwich to me.

I shook my head. "No, I'm good. But, thanks."

"I been meaning to ask you something," Crow said after he swallowed a huge bite of the sandwich. "Your nipples. Are they a light brown like caramel? Or more a dark chocolate, like a Hershey's Kiss?"

My mouth fell open at the audacity of such a personal question, especially while my boyfriend sat just behind me. But then again, I'd just watched this man fuck another man's girl in a filthy, arousing, acrobatic, hot way while her boyfriend and my boyfriend watched.

"Owl won't tell," Crow said after the final bite of his sandwich. "He said I had to wait for you to show me. Can I see for myself?"

My finger went to the top button of my shirt. I had no clue if I was about to clutch the fabric surrounding the button or pull it open. I didn't know what I wanted to do?

I looked to Owl, the man who for the last few weeks had complete control over my pleasure. Owl shrugged, leaving the decision entirely up to me.

I looked to Ellie who lay with her head resting against Hawk's heart, his fingers twined around hers. Ellie tore her gaze from Hawk and regarded me. Her eyebrow tilted up in that challenging way, just like Owl's did. In fact they all seemed able to do that eyebrow tilt thing. Looking around the room, there were five eyebrows tilting up at me.

"If you show him your tits," said Eagle. "I get to see your pussy."

My index finger circled the plastic button of my shirt. "Is this some sort of initiation to the gang?"

"We're not a gang." Crow laid his head on my breasts and looked up at me with puppy eyes. "We're just friends." He leaned his head over to poke with his nose behind the flap of my shirt. "I'm guessing they're Hershey's Kisses. I could suck on Hershey's Kiss all day long."

Eagle came and sat on the coffee table before me. "We've all shown you ours, Kira. Show us yours."

SIXTEEN

They waited patiently for me to pop open every button of my shirt. Once the last clasp was free, Crow spread the edges apart and down my arms. He inclined his head at my bra. Though Eagle may have used a bit of peer pressure to get my shirt open, I knew that no one would force me to do anything I didn't truly want to do. I undid my bra and let it fall off my chest.

"Look at that," sighed Crow. "They're dark like Kisses. Can I kiss them Kira?"

"I..."

Crow stuck out his tongue and took a swipe at one of my nipples. "Tell me to stop if you don't like it," he said around a mouthful.

I gasped as both my nipples instantly hardened

into tight points. Owl gave my breasts plenty of attention on a regular basis, but there was something about Crow's tongue that was...different.

I looked down as Crow took another taste. He curled his tongue in a way I can't describe. Then he flattened it out and circled my entire areola. A low moan escaped me as I tried to keep my eyes open and watch his technique.

"I think she likes it." Eagle leaned back on the table.

My head dipped back, and I saw Owl's chin. I stiffened for a moment, fearful that he'd get angry at my reaction to another man's touch.

Owl leaned down and smiled at me. He planted a light kiss on my lips. My head rolled into the middle of his chest and I heard his heartbeat. It was in tune with mine.

As Crow switched to the other breast, Eagle parted my thighs. He reached for the elastic of my panties, and with Owl's help in lifting my hips, Eagle slid my panties off and put them in his pocket. Then he knelt down on the ground and disappeared under my skirt.

"I love the contrast of a chocolate pussy," he said. "Brown and pink are a fucking hot combination. My favorite is brown, pink, and the white from a girl coming. It's like a Neapolitan ice cream sundae." Eagle's head reappeared. "I'm gonna make you cream, Kira. That cool with you?"

My response was gurgled as Crow chose that moment to suck my nipple hard.

Eagle rolled up my skirt. He reached into a side table drawer and pulled out two sex toys. Neither were the long traditional dildos I'd seen before. Neither were they like the small vibe Owl had gifted me at the beginning of our relationship.

"You get in that ass, yet?"

I realized Eagle was talking to Owl.

"No, but she likes to be rimmed. She's had anal sex before but she's never liked it."

Owl and I had never talked about that, but like all things to do with my pleasure he somehow knew.

"She will tonight." Eagle grabbed some lube and rubbed it on my asshole. I squirmed at his touch, but in a good way.

He held up a small, squat dildo with a stoppered end. He looked me dead in the eye as he oiled it, waiting for an objection. I realized the dildo looked so different than anything I'd seen before because it wasn't for the vagina.

I opened my mouth. I had no idea what I was

about to say, but it didn't matter. No words came out. Crow chose that moment to bite my nipple.

They all chuckled as I bucked and jerked. Though they were using toys on me for my pleasure, I felt like I was the shiny, new toy that everyone wanted to play with and use for their pleasure.

Eagle swirled the butt plug around my anus. Owl was right. I liked ass play, the rimming part where he'd flick his tongue down past my clit, past my pussy, over that patch of skin that connected my pussy and my anus, and then finally flick open my back door.

That tiny patch of skin that was my anus had more nerves than my clit. Owl would have me dancing around the bed as he laved over it. None of my exes had bothered much with that. I'd been thankful in the past when they at least oiled me up before venturing inside that entrance. Eagle played, teasing with me, until I felt my ass hole puckering like a thirsty baby.

I felt fingers grazing my temple. Owl stared down at me, a light, thoughtful smile on his face. He brushed his thumb across my eyebrow, then over my cheekbone.

I forgot that another man was about to push a dildo up my ass. I forgot that yet another tongued my left tit. I wasn't even thinking about the couple sitting off to the side watching the whole exchange go down. My entire world narrowed on Owl as I lay against his chest with pleasure swirling all around me.

I felt such a connection to him in that moment. Even though his hands barely touched me, I felt like he held my soul in a secure grip that would never break. I felt like his soul was wrapped around mine. We were entwined and nothing could ever break us apart.

"Ahh," I reared up as Eagle slid the butt plug home. It wasn't a thick plug, nor was it a long device. The tip was a soft arrowhead that fed into a more bulbous center that narrowed again at the end. It was the bulbous part that my mind focused on. I clenched around it involuntarily.

A buzzing sound broke my concentration. I looked up to see Eagle with the second sex toy. This one was a wand. It looked like a dental instrument; the mirror the hygienist would put in your mouth to see your wisdom teeth. But this toy didn't have a mirror. It had a small, curved head that was shaped much like the dildo presently inside my ass. Only this one vibrated.

Eagle's eyes connected with mine. He waited

again for me to object. Part of me wondered if he wanted me to say no.

Would he force me into submission? Was that his thing? Well, he would not have those dark needs met tonight. My thighs relaxed open. My channel was already dripping wet from Crow's constant suckling of my breasts. Eagle would need no lube for my pussy.

At first contact of the vibe, I jerked. Eagle left it there until I relaxed into the buzz. The moment my breathing normalized, he pushed it into me.

I thought he'd put the whole vibe into me. But he didn't. In fact, he couldn't. The device was shaped at such an angle it could only go in a short distance.

I frowned. Exactly how was this short-ended dildo going to get me off? Little did I know...

Like a doctor manipulating one of his instruments, Eagle maneuvered the vibe around inside my channel. It wasn't comfortable. It wasn't pleasurable. I was about to open my mouth in protest until-

"There it is."

Eagle pressed the vibe upwards, into the front wall of my pussy. I dug my heels into the couch and arched my pussy into the device as it drilled into my G-spot. In a matter of seconds I went from the bottom of a cliff to the top of a mountain of pleasure. I only held on by my pinkie toe.

But I didn't want to hold on. I wanted to be flung over the edge into the oblivion of pleasure that had built inside of me.

The combination of Crow grazing his teeth over my nipples, of Eagle pressing firm with that vibe, and of Owl gently stroking my temple, not to mention the pressure in my ass, all of these were forces pressing against my back, urging me to jump, to leap. But I couldn't let go.

There were ticks happening all over my body. The fingers of my left hand shook uncontrollably as though a fault line were cracking it open. My right knee bounced up and down. My chest shook. Parts of my body were cracking at the seams, trying to get the orgasm to come out of me. But the cracks and fissures weren't enough. I needed more. I needed something more.

"You wanna come, baby?"

I looked up at Owl. That was what I needed; for him to say the words. He'd begun this whole adventure into bliss. I couldn't go any further without him.

"Come for me, Kira."

And just like that, my body released the pressure that Eagle and Crow had built up in me. It was a massive explosion as everything gushed out of me.

"Fuck, man," groaned Eagle. "You didn't tell me your girl fucking squirts."

I had felt more wetness than usual leave me. I peeled open one eyelid and saw a puddle of fluid on the leather couch. I was mortified. Had I peed in front of these guys?

"Ooh, I want a taste." Crow let go of my breasts and moved between my thighs. He lapped up the liquid. Then he looked up at me and grinned. "Sweet as berries. Do it again, E. I wanna see this time."

"All right. Fuck her ass." Eagle indicated the butt plug.

Crow took hold of the end of the plug and thrust it in and out of me. They were small movements, but they felt like he was ramming all the way into me. My ass grabbed at the plug and squeezed each time he brought it back into me.

In my pussy, Eagle found that spot just inside my front wall again. He stroked harder, faster. That same pressure built up again, instantaneously. My hips shook as it battered against me to get out. This time I felt the fluid get called down. Some of it leaked out of me in anticipation. The pressure was delicious. My eyes rolled back in my head and landed on Owl.

Owl looked at me in wonder, like I was the most precious thing in the world. I studied his face, focused on his lips, waiting for him to give me that final push. He entwined his fingers with my own.

"Come for me, baby," he whispered in my ear.

I let go of everything. Everything I was. Everything I thought. Everything I thought I wanted to be. There was only this, only him.

As my body released, Owl brought my face up to him and captured my cries. "You're the most beautiful thing I've ever seen in my life, Kira."

SEVENTEEN

A few hours later, I woke up alone in Owl's bed. From the one window in his room, I saw that the sun was still out but starting to set. I stretched my limbs and felt the throbbing buzz that came as a result of a good work out. I smiled to myself. I had been worked out pretty good.

As soon as I had the thought I wiped the smile away. I'd just let two other guys fuck me. Not fuck me in the biblical sense with their own cocks, but they'd sure as hell touched me in every place where my bathing suit went.

I let the name *slut* whisper into my brain. I waited in stillness for it to stick. I waited in silence to greet the shame.

Neither happened. It may have sounded crazy,

but the truth was that Eagle and Crow had been nothing but respectful as they'd fucked me with their fingers, mouths, and toys.

I didn't feel like a slut. I didn't feel ashamed. I kinda wanted to do it again.

I got up from Owl's bed. He'd laid me under his covers naked, but he'd laid out my clothes across one of the chairs in his room. I put my clothes back on. Then I froze. Out of the corner of my eye, sitting on his night table, was his cellphone.

I warred with myself for a good two minutes before old habits won out. I snatched up the device preparing to crack the code that would get me into his social media, emails, and texts. I glanced at the closed door to the basement, unsure how much time I'd have for my sleuthing. I swiped my thumb across the screen and... what the hell?

There was no passcode. His basic blue screen displaying all his apps came up. I could click any app and it would open to me.

I looked up at the closed door again. Was this some kind of test? Was he laying in wait to catch me? Did he plant a fake text or email from a girl to see if I'd try to catch him? Or... or did he simply have nothing to hide from me?

I sat the phone back on his side table. I climbed

the steps in a daze. The first person I saw in the early evening light was Ellie. She sat at the dining room table, fully clothed with her textbooks open.

She looked up and smiled. "Hey, Shakira. You have a good nap?"

It was strange to look her in the eye. We'd seen each other naked. We'd seen each other's ecstasy faces. I wasn't ashamed, but I still dipped my head down instead of looking her directly in the eye when I answered.

"Hey, sis." I had to clear my throat before more words could get out. "Where is every body?"

"They're all across the street in the shop. You want some pancakes? Hawk made them."

"Your boyfriend cooks?"

"They all cook." Ellie got up and made me a plate. "And your boyfriend is obsessive about cleaning. I thought this place would be a mess, and they'd expect me to be their maid. But I have yet to touch a pot, pan, or broom. I don't think I'll ever leave."

I accepted the plate of pancakes Ellie sat down before me and took a seat at the table. "You live here?"

"Practically, but not yet. After graduation."

Hawk's pancakes were delicious, fluffy and

sweet. I finished half of the serving before asking the next question, the one I really wanted to know.

"So, you and Hawk are pretty serious? How do you manage not getting jealous watching him with other women?"

"The first time I saw him with someone else was not fun." Ellie's eyes narrowed in memory. "But after that... I don't know? He looks over at me when he's with someone else, like it's almost a game and he wants me to see how well he's doing at it. Or like he wants me to see what he's going to do to me later. That probably sounds really messed up."

I was no longer sure if it was messed up. Instead of responding, I put the last bit of pancake into my mouth.

"He always makes me feel included," Ellie continued. "Even when he goes off and is alone with someone else. He always comes back and tells me about it -if I want to hear. There's never anything to hide between us. It makes me feel safe with him, like I don't have to worry about surprises."

I pushed the empty plate away from me and chanced a look at Ellie's face. "I've been cheated on before. A lot of times, really. With every boyfriend I've ever had, actually."

"People cheat when they're unsatisfied or denied something they want."

Well, that was a slap in the face.

"No, no," Ellie sighed and tried again. "I know because I cheated before; on my boyfriend before Hawk. We weren't right for each other and I didn't know that. Maybe none of those other guys were right for you, and they knew it? Maybe you knew it too? Maybe you kept only choosing guys who were wrong for you because you didn't know what the right guy looked like? Maybe now you do and that won't happen any more?"

I held my breath while Ellie contemplated her next words. I leaned in, my eyes not breaking contact with her face now.

"From what I know, and what I've seen, Owl has been nothing but loyal to you. He told me about you the first time we were... introduced. He's surrounded by temptations and invitations every night. But since I've known him, he's always told them all that he has a girl."

Ellie's words filled me up like cracking the code of an exes phone and finding no new texts or friend requests used to do. Her words validated every hope, wish, and prayer I had about my relationship with Owl, more than his words ever could.

Now, that was pretty messed up. The fact that I could trust someone else's word so easily over my boyfriend's. A boyfriend who'd given me no reason to distrust him. A boyfriend who'd held and kissed me while I came at the hands of two of his friends. A boyfriend who didn't show an ounce of jealousy or anxiety when I was out of his sight. A boyfriend who left nothing locked up or hidden in my presence.

The back door opened and one by one the entire crew filed in. Hawk, who had been jabbing at Eagle, failed to duck a punch and got it in his arm. Hawk lunged for Eagle, but Eagle ducked behind Ellie as a shield. Hawk gave up his pursuit and reached for Ellie instead, bending her back and kissing her.

Eagle chuckled, left them, and came over and picked up my empty plate and utensils. "You good?" His eyes studied my face.

I nodded. He winked at me and brought my dirty dishes over to the sink.

Crow spotted me and wrapped me up in a bear hug. "Hey, Kira. I'm making pasta for dinner. You like pesto?"

"Yeah," I said into the cushion of his chest. "That sounds good."

Crow gave my shoulder a squeeze and went to the fridge to pull out the ingredients he needed.

Owl came in last. He leaned into Ellie's ear and whispered something. Ellie giggled, turning her head towards him. Hawk jabbed towards him, but Owl ducked away laughing.

Owl pulled a chair up behind me, draped his arms over my chair, and rested one hand against my heart. The other hand he used to make rude gestures at Eagle as they continued whatever argument they all had been having prior to coming into the house.

"You good, Kira?" Owl whispered in my ear.

I leaned my head back against his heart and closed my eyes. "Yeah, I'm good."

EIGHTEEN

With my belly full from Crow's pesto pasta, I followed Owl down into the basement to get my purse and prepare to leave for the night. Owl jogged down the steps, in a great mood after good food and good conversation with his friends. I slogged down the steps, taking one at a time. My fingers alternately curled around the banister and then straightened to glide over it.

"Owl?"

"Yeah, baby?"

"You want to fuck Ellie, right?"

He stopped in his tracks and turned to look at me. His face screwed into a puzzle as though I were asking him a trick question.

I took the last step that put me onto the ground level. "I think I would be okay with that."

Owl quirked that eyebrow up. "You *think*?"

I swallowed, gathering my courage. "I would be okay with it. But," I took a deep breath. "But I would need something in return."

Owl waited, watching me. His feet were planted apart in a firm stance. His arms were crossed over his chest. His face was impassive as he regarded me.

"I want to sleep with you. I mean *sleep* sleep. In your bed. With you. Afterwards." I waited a moment for him to soak in all those caveats before I endeavored to explain any further. "I think if I could establish that closeness with you after watching you be intimate with another woman I would be okay with it."

Owl unfolded his arms and brought me into them. "Kira, I'm not this close to any other woman. You mean more to me than anybody else."

I took a moment, closed my eyes, and allowed those words to seep into my consciousness. "I hear you say those words. My logical brain takes them in, but my heart has trouble accepting it." I opened my eyes, hoping this would make him see. "I've just had too many bad experiences to accept it at face value. I'm sorry."

Owl sighed, placing both hands on the sides of my cheeks. He tilted my face up so that he could plant a light kiss on my eyelids. "You don't have to apologize for what someone else did to you."

"I'm trying, Owl. I'm trying so hard because I want this to work between us. I want it more than anything. But I need this one thing. For you to hold me, so I feel close to you. So I don't feel alone."

He circled his arms around me and rested his head on top of mine. I knew he was thinking about it. I knew what his answer would be as our heartbeats fell into sync with one another.

"Deal," he said.

I let out a breath I hadn't known I'd ben holding and pulled back so I could see his face. "So, I can stay tonight?"

He blinked. "You want me to fuck her now?"

I nodded. "You probably should before I chicken out. Show me that there's nothing to worry about."

<hr>

THIS WAS A FIRST FOR ME. I was watching my boyfriend finger fuck another girl without going into a blind rage. And even more interesting, I was sitting next to the girl-in-question's boyfriend. Crow and Eagle had left for the evening, off to some other form of debauchery. It was just the two couples left in the house.

Owl had knocked on Hawk's bedroom door just fifteen minutes ago and explained what we were doing there. After Owl made his request, Hawk looked over his shoulder at a lounging Ellie. Ellie rose from the bed and eagerly accepted Owl's request. They brought in two chairs, shut the door, and Owl went to Ellie on the bed.

Owl wasn't exactly finger fucking Ellie. He was giving her a massage with oils. I guess it was kind of him. After all, she'd just spent an hour fucking two other guys this afternoon, and likely had then come to her bedroom and fucked her boyfriend. Now, she had her legs spread for my boyfriend.

That word whispered across my mind again as I looked at Ellie: *slut*. But still, it didn't stick or leave behind any of its shame. Ellie was my friend and, believe it or not, she was doing me a favor.

Here I was falling for a guy who liked to fuck other women. Both Owl and Ellie had offered me words to calm my fears. Now, the two of them were trying to show me with actions that I had nothing to be afraid of.

Owl squirted more oil into his hands and then

spread it over Ellie's abdomen. The entire room smelled of lavender and vanilla. I chanced a glance at Hawk, who sat beside me in a folding chair. I now knew the sight of his girl getting fucked wasn't an issue for him, but I wasn't so sure how he felt about having his room smell like a perfumery.

Hawk sat in a pair of boxer shorts with his legs outstretched and his arms crossed over his chest. He looked slightly annoyed. "Owl, are you gonna fuck her or what? I could've paid for a masseuse."

"Just relax, man." Owl knelt between Ellie's opened legs. "Her body's taken a beating. You don't want me pounding into her and making her sore."

Hawk huffed like a toddler and shifted in his seat.

"Breathe for me, Ellie." Owl's hands followed the path of Ellie's breath, massaging up her diaphragm as she inhaled and then down and around her belly as she exhaled. "Would you like to come again, Ellie?"

"Yeah," she said. "But I don't think I can."

Owl smiled. "Just relax and let me do all the work. I'll get you there, I promise."

Ellie smiled and closed her eyes, her entire body relaxed and opened. She clearly trusted Owl. Owl made small taps on Ellie's pubic bone.

"Is this some Japanese voodoo shit?"

Owl grinned without turning to answer Hawk. "It's samurai magic. Now, shut the fuck up while I make your girl see stars."

I thought for sure, Hawk would jump out of his seat. But the thought of Ellie coming hard enough to see stars was a welcome idea to both him and his girlfriend. He sat back in his seat and was quiet for a few more minutes while Owl continued his massage of Ellie's genital area.

Owl spread Ellie's legs wider, likely for Hawk's and my viewing pleasure. His fingers made direct contact with Ellie's clitoris and labia. They lightly massaged her already plump lips and swollen clit.

I heard Ellie's breathing pattern change. Her hips jerked slightly trying to anticipate Owl's touch. He didn't speed up his manipulations. He didn't firm his touch. He pulled Ellie's outer lips apart and gently massaged those. He looked alternately at what he was doing between her legs and at her face to gage her reaction.

I knew he was aroused. I could see it, but there was nothing lustful or lecherous in Owl's eyes. He was attentive to his charge.

His eyes caught mine. A smile spread across his

face. There, in his glance at me, I saw it. The lust he didn't give to Ellie.

Owl wanted Ellie. I knew that. But when he looked at me... it was different. I couldn't explain that look in his eyes and how it flicked to something else when it landed on me. It was like turning an overhead light on in a room lit by moonlight.

"Owl if you don't get started soon I'm gonna come over there and finish it for you." Hawk growled.

"We're almost there," soothed Owl. "Aren't we, Ellie?"

Ellie's response was a shuddered breath. Her hips undulated even more.

"Okay, I think we're there." Owl reached over to the nightstand and grabbed a condom. He tore open the packet with his teeth. As he rolled it on, his eyes caught mine again. He held his dick in his hand and raised an eyebrow.

I realized that he was asking me for permission. *Last chance*, that look said. *Are you in or out?*

I nodded my head.

When Owl turned away and slid into Ellie, I gulped. Beside me, Hawk smirked. He put his hand on my shoulder and gave me a squeeze. Then we both turned our attention back to the bed.

"Oh fuck, Ellie. Your meat's still pretty sweet, isn't it?"

Ellie grinned up at Owl.

Hawk let out a laugh.

I felt a twinge of disappointment at being left out of whatever private joke they were sharing. But the twinge left me as I watched Owl's penis disappear into Ellie.

He fucked her slow, with deep strokes that had his ass cheeks clenching as he tilted up and into her. Ellie trembled and groaned with an impending orgasm. She was on the cliff, about to step over into oblivion when Owl withdrew.

"Owl, watch how much you tease my girl," Hawk warned.

Owl ignored Hawk and flipped Ellie onto her stomach. With Ellie up on her knees in Doggy Style, he entered her from behind. He thrust into her, slow and ass-clenchingly deep just like before.

Owl reached around and grabbed both of Ellie's arms, bringing them behind her back. He sped up his thrusting, still pumping deeply into her. Ellie's face went into the mattress, raising her ass up higher in the air. Ellie whimpered, her body and mind in that place of suspension at the top of the roller coaster ride.

"Owl…" Hawk's tone was a low growl.

Owl's eyes came back to me, a question. He was asking me if I should let her come. I'd been where Ellie was more times than I could count. I thought I hated it, thought it was a place of denial. But it wasn't. That place of suspension was where I saw everything clearly just before everything crashed around me and I lost all sense.

I waited one breath, two, three, before I nodded to Owl, giving him the go ahead. I thought he would pump faster into Ellie, but he slowed down. I watched Ellie's body shake, starting at her hips, and then radiating out to her legs and her torso.

The orgasm broke from her on a scream that anyone not in the room might've thought was one of pain. The orgasm continued with long, low moans as her body quivered and quaked. Ellie came so hard for so long she pushed Owl out of her. She shook and jerked on the bed as though she were having a seizure.

Owl knelt over her, watchful and attentive to her every move.

And finally, the convulsions turned down to the more normal trembling of post-orgasmic bliss. Ellie curled herself into a fetal position while she caught her breath.

When her eyes opened, they were slow to focus. But finally she did, and a lazy smile spread across her face. "Thanks, Owl."

Owl grinned back at her. "You're welcome, sweet meat."

"Fuck," Hawk whispered beside me. He looked as shell-shocked as Ellie. His dick was ramrod straight in his boxer shorts.

Owl wrapped Ellie in a blanket and carried her to Hawk. "After that, I need to fucking blow. Do you mind?" Owl tilted his head to indicate the bed.

"Nah," said Hawk. "Knock yourself out man."

Owl crooked his finger at me. I looked down. His dick was rock hard and pointing up at me.

NINETEEN

"You didn't come?" I asked.

Owl shook his head. "I only come for you."

All my life I've heard stories about people falling in love. I thought I'd been in love before. I'd tripped over some douche bags, fallen down on top of their shit, and gotten hurt by them. Not this time.

I took Owl's hand and allowed him to pull me up. This time, I stepped into love with sure feet. Owl fell backwards onto Hawk's bed and I climbed on top of him. He caught me as I descended down onto him for a kiss.

Owl reached between us and removed the condom he'd just used with Ellie. He reached for another, but I stayed his hand. "You don't have to. I'm clean and on the pill. And I trust you."

I reached under my skirt to slide my panties to the side, only to remember that Eagle had never given them back from this afternoon. I hitched my skirt up over my ass and sat down on the dick of the man I loved.

Owl let his head fall back onto the pillows. He rubbed his thumb over my lip and let me ride him. We stared into each other's eyes as we filled and expanded into each other.

There it was, what had been missing in his eyes when he'd fucked Ellie. That look of lust mixed with something I hoped and prayed was love. Looking directly into it right now, I saw a spotlight in the darkness that had been inside of me all of my life. It was so bright I had to look away.

I laid my head down on Owl's shoulder as I continued to ride him. He rested one hand gently in my hair and the other went to my ass. He rimmed me with his fingers, inserting one into my anus.

His thrusts sped up, and he pumped into me harder, pulling me down onto him. "Fuck, Kira, fuck," he panted. "I'm sorry, baby."

I pulled away to look into his eyes, trying to understand what he was sorry for. His face contorted in that picture of agony and ecstasy that was orgasm. It was beautiful. I couldn't take my eyes off him as he jerked and spilled his seed into me.

With his last jerk, he collapsed back onto the bed. "Shit, baby I'm sorry. I didn't let you come."

I let out a low laugh. Was that all? Didn't he realize that without his loving I would've spent my life faking my way through sex and relationships? Owl had set me free, taught me to soar. One missed ride was nothing in the face of that.

"Don't worry, man. I got her." I looked behind me as Hawk stood and deposited a swaddled Ellie in one of the chairs. Then he made his way over, his thick erection leading the way.

I looked to Owl who was still slightly dazed from his orgasm. He raised that eyebrow at me, but it wasn't in challenge. I knew if I gave him the word, he'd take me out of here. I looked back at Hawk. Not at Hawk, at Hawk's dick. It was thick and long and it made me... curious.

Owl chuckled beneath me. He rolled me over, planting a deep kiss on my lips. Then he rose from the bed and made his way over to Ellie and the vacant seat.

Hawk grabbed a condom and rolled it on his massive dick. Then he came behind me. We lay on our sides and he wrapped his big body around me in a spoon and faced us both so we were looking at our loved ones. Owl reached out an arm to Ellie, and she leaned into him, resting her head on his shoulder.

Hawk entered my pussy from behind. No foreplay, no preamble. He let his cockhead part my lips and took his time sliding into me. I was thankful he gave me time to get used to him. I had no complaints about the size of my man's instrument, but I had to admit Hawk's dick was in another category.

My eyes widened as Hawk made his way damn near into my belly. Owl grinned back at me, not an ounce of jealousy on his face. He reminded me of how Hawk looked when Eagle or Crow fucked Ellie. Like it was a thing of beauty.

I kept my eyes on Owl as Hawk fucked into me. Hawk was not gentle. He fucked me hard, slapping his hips against my ass. My brain cells were near fried, but I remembered him saying he liked it rough from time to time. Every guy I'd ever been with before Owl had taken me pretty roughly. But there was something different about the way Hawk moved his hips into me.

He spread my thighs wide, opening me up to his thrusting. He played with my clitoris, making slow, light circles in opposition to his hard, fast thrusting.

Any remaining brain cells I had sizzled in the heat between us.

We grunted together in a two-part harmony. I felt myself approaching the top of the cliff, but I knew I wouldn't get over by myself. I opened my eyes and focused on my boyfriend.

Owl's eyes were watchful and attentive on me. He knew what I needed. He nodded his head for me to proceed.

I still couldn't go over. It wasn't enough. I looked to him desperately, trying to communicate to him that I needed the words, needed him to tell me to do it.

"Come for me, Kira."

I closed my eyes and melted back into Hawk as I slid down that slippery mountain of bliss. Hawk was not too far behind me.

* * *

I'D FALLEN asleep in Owl's arms. We'd left Ellie and Hawk alone in their room and made our way back down into the basement. We washed up in a warm shower and then slipped under the covers naked. Owl cocooned himself around my body, twining his legs and his hands with my own. I felt safe, protected, at home.

I woke in the middle of the night to him stroking my hair.

"Do you need some space?"

Those words were hard for me to force out. I did not want to leave, but even more than that I didn't want him to leave me. If this were the thing that would push him away, me insisting on sleeping in his bed, I'd give it up and go back to sleeping alone. I'd been doing it most of my life. Lying in a cold bed would be worth the price of admission into this man's heart.

"No, I'm good," he said. "This is comfortable."

I breathed a sigh of relief as he ran his fingers through my hair.

"Hey, Owl?"

"Yeah, baby?"

"That thing you did with Ellie, the massage, I want you to do that to me."

"I will, baby," I heard the smile in his voice. "Tomorrow night, okay?"

"Okay."

"Go back to sleep, Kira."

It was the best night of sleep I'd had in years, probably the best night of sleep of my life. Most of my nights as a child I'd awakened to shouts of anger or cries of despair. I'd lay awake in the dark, alone. Aching for someone to hold me through the night. But my mother was not the affectionate type, at least not with her child. And my father was never around. He'd never paid me enough attention to reach his arms out to me. But none of that mattered any more.

I woke up late the next morning. It was near ten when I rolled over. Owl wasn't in bed, but I wasn't surprised at that after I saw the time. He had done more than enough. He'd held me through the night, keeping me warm and safe. I think he kissed me at sunrise before he slipped out. It may have been a dream, but I was leaning more towards it being reality.

I rose and pulled on yesterday's clothes, which were laid out neatly again. The house was empty when I made my way upstairs. Peering out the window to the front of the house, I saw that even Ellie's car was gone. She was likely in the lab getting ready for finals. I should be in the library getting my last bit of studying on before exams started. And then I would be headed back home for the summer.

That thought did not sit well with me. The last thing I wanted to do was leave Owl. I had money saved from my part time job. Maybe I could rent an apartment for the summer. Maybe I could just stay here for the summer.

I texted Owl, asking where he was.

He responded immediately, telling me he was in the garage.

I made my way over there. There was loud music playing, practically bouncing off the walls. I opened the door to see a woman splayed out on the hood of a car. Eagle fucked her pussy. Crow had his dick between her breasts. Hawk had his dick in her mouth. And then there was Owl, who had his fingers on her clit.

I froze on the spot.

They were all laughing and saying filthy things to the woman, who I could see was a full grown woman and not some coed from one of their parties. Hawk had his massive dick rammed all the way down her throat in what looked like a painful way. Eagle slammed into her pussy in a way that reminded me of every one of my ex-boyfriends. Crow pinched her nipples hard as he fucked the valley of her breasts. Owl flicked his fingers on her swollen clit.

He must have sensed my presence because he looked up at me. With the woman's clit still in hand, he smiled. It was a playful smile; a smile that said look at how I'm winning at this game I'm playing. He didn't wrench his hands away and try to hide what he was doing.

I turned and dashed out of the door.

I burst out of the garage and into the sun trying to catch my breath.

"Kira?" He yelled after me. "Baby, what's wrong?" He caught up and turned me around to face him.

"How could you do that?" I sniffed.

"Do what?"

Tears streamed down my face as I looked up at him realizing he would deny what I'd just seen with my own eyes. "You cheated on me. Just like all the rest of them. How could you fuck another woman after all that's happened between us?"

"What are you talking about?"

I tried to wrench myself out of his hands, but he wouldn't let me go. I yanked out of his hold and jerked back when he reached for me again.

I couldn't listen to him anymore. He'd twist what I saw away from reality. He'd make me believe him and his vision. If I didn't get away now I'd fall for it. I'd fall hard for it. The type of hurt that Owl could deal me would be the type I might never recover from.

I'd wind up just like my mother; sitting alone, staring out a window, waiting for someone to show up only to have him disappear again for weeks, months at a time. That would not be me. I swore that would never be me. I had to get out of here.

"Kira," Owl called after me. "Kira, stop."

I didn't. I couldn't. I had to get away or else I would fall and never get back up. I'd lie back down in his bed and never bring myself to get back out of it.

"Kira, come for me. Now."

I almost laughed out loud. Yeah, right. Like that's going to-

I nearly doubled over as my body responded to his command. Like an arrow, I shot up the mountain. I didn't pause at the top. I came crashing down to my knees right there on the street.

I couldn't stop it. I couldn't end it. I dug my nails into the dirt and waited for the orgasm to stop. It was not pleasant. In fact, it hurt. I sobbed my way through it until it was over.

A hand reached out and touched my shoulder. I turned and smacked it away.

"Don't touch me," I snarled. "Don't you ever touch me again. Don't you ever talk to me again."

I covered my ears and took off at a run.

TWENTY

I woke up alone in my childhood bed. I'd been home many times before over the two years I'd been away at college, but this morning was the first time the bed felt too small for my body. There were lumps in the mattress I hadn't noticed before. The room smelled stuffy as though my mother kept the doors and windows closed.

My clit throbbed in need of attention. I'd left the vibe back in my dorm room. The constant aching had kept me awake all night. Sometime around three in the morning, I reached my hand between my thighs to answer its cries.

I didn't start slow. There was no teasing. My strokes were a full on assault of my pussy. It was part frustration, part anger, part desperation to get my body under control; back under my control.

I rubbed myself vigorously, trying to keep my mind blank of any and all thought. I only allowed myself to feel. To feel my slippery fingers on the terrain of my pussy as I stirred it to life. I got close. Closer than I'd ever gotten before on my own.

I scrambled up that cliff by sheer force of will. At the top I thrust my fingers into my pussy and pushed myself up the cliff. But I faltered at the edge, looking down at the place I so desperately wanted to be, the place I so desperately needed to be.

I rocked my hips along with the movements of my hand inching myself closer and closer to the edge. I thought about all the times I'd been flung off that cliff into oblivion. I mimicked the panting sounds of falling. I imitated the guttural sounds of crashing into bliss.

And then, it happened.

A tiny tremor broke free from my core. It was small, but it was enough. My pussy clenched around that tremor, stoking its embers. Tears stung my eyes as I let out a half groan, half laugh at my accomplishment.

"Kira? You awake?"

I wrenched my hand out of my panties. "Yeah, Momma. I'll be out in a minute."

I waited until I heard my mother's footsteps go down the hall before I got out of bed. I changed my underwear, pulling the fabric over my happy pussy. It may have been a small treat, but it was a big deal to me. It proved I didn't need him after all, which was good because it appeared I never had him in the first place.

I looked over to my cell phone on my nightstand. The flashing lights indicated that I had voice messages, texts, and emails that were unanswered. I left the phone there, untouched, and headed out of my bedroom.

I walked out into the living room where my mother sat by the window, a cigarette in between her fingers. She took a long pull as she looked out of the window at the empty street. Her other hand rested on a house phone.

"Hey, Momma."

"You want breakfast?"

"No, Momma. I was thinking about taking a walk."

"Okay, pick up a pack of Kools for me."

"Why don't you come with me?"

My mother tore her eyes away from the window.

Her fingers grasped the phone. "You know I can't leave, Shakira. What if your father calls and needs me to come pick him up? What if I'm not here when he comes home?" She pulled the phone into her lap and turned back to the window, taking another pull of her cigarette. "He forgot his key the last time he left. I don't want to leave just to have to run back home. Like I always told you, a man isn't really yours if you have to chase after him. Why don't you sit with me for a while?"

I sat down in the folding chair beside her, not the comforter opposite her; that was my father's chair. Its cushions were plump as though it hadn't been sat in for weeks, maybe months this time. I had no idea the last time my father returned home this year.

My mother kept this place exactly as it had been when my dad lived here full time. No additions of trinkets, no subtractions of anything. She sat bound to that chair with no ropes, not even a voice command. My father didn't care if she came or went. But she chose to always be here just in case he called or stopped by because a real woman always stood by her man, even if he wasn't there.

I shook my mother's voice out of my head. "I gotta get back to campus, Momma. Exams are coming up."

She nodded her head, her attention focused off in the distance up the street. I doubt it registered when I walked out the door.

I TURNED in my biology exam, certain I'd aced it. I'd spouted a lot of bullshit about natural selection and the Theory of Super Fecundity. To solve Darwin's issues of organisms producing more offspring than what's required to replace themselves, I recommended that the world adapt to a polyamorous model of matriarchy where one woman would mate with a number of males. She could only have one to two offspring at any one time. If none of the males were sure of the paternity then they'd all be compelled to care for the woman and the child. To prove my theory, I pointed to bees, which my biology tutor, Ellie, had pointed to as an example early in our sessions. I was certain my Biology 101 professor, who was an older female, would get a kick out of the paper if nothing else.

With that over, I made my way out of the classroom and ran into Ellie. She was dressed in jean shorts and a t-shirt. I realized I'd never seen her out of knee length skirts... or naked.

"How are you?" she asked.

I shrugged, not wanting to discuss my break up. Ellie reached out for my shoulder. I let her touch me, not realizing until she did how much I needed the contact.

"If you need somebody to talk to, I'm here," she said. "I doubt any of your other girlfriends would understand the choices you made in the last few weeks."

I didn't really have other girlfriends. I'd never trusted them to not try and steal my man. I looked at Ellie with her trusting blue eyes and friendly smile. It was the same smile she'd given me when she agreed to fuck my boyfriend to show me that there was nothing to worry about in sharing sexual partners. I should feel angry with her for opening the door and then her legs, but I didn't. She'd only been trying to help then. I believed she was trying to help me now.

"I thought he was different," I said. "I thought if we kept everything out in the open I wouldn't get hurt. But he lied to me. He cheated on me just like all the others."

Ellie led me to a bench under a tree. "When you say he cheated, what do you mean exactly?"

"He fucked another woman. It's the one thing

we agreed he would not do -without my okay first. I was trying to live his lifestyle. I did everything he asked. And he couldn't keep it in his pants."

"Did he actually take it out of his pants with this other woman?" Ellie asked.

"He was playing with her clit. Fondling is fucking in my book."

"I'm not discounting what you feel," Ellie said, rubbing my shoulder. "But I think you should talk to him. I suspect fondling is not in his definition of fucking."

"All men are just selfish, immature, and incapable of commitment. This whole fuck-my-friends thing is just a cover to fuck whoever he wants without taking any responsibility. I thought I could deal with it. How do you do it?"

Ellie leaned back against the bench and thought about her answer before giving it to me. "It's not that I don't get angry or jealous when Hawk's with somebody else. I didn't when he was with you because I know you. I feel more comfortable when he's fucking somebody I know."

"Well, I'm sorry, sis, but I don't think I'll be fucking your boyfriend again any time soon. I don't think I'll be fucking any man again anytime soon. It's times like these that I wish I were a lesbian."

Ellie chuckled. "I'm sure lesbians have the same problems as heterosexuals. What I've realized is that when I'm feeling a way about Hawk having sex with someone else it's rarely his fault."

I recoiled at her statement.

Ellie held up her hands in a stop motion. "Just listen for a sec. When I get jealous or angry it's usually because of something I'm insecure about. If we argue, and we have, it's never about sex. Maybe I feel like another girl is more attractive than me. Or she has better moves. And that all might be true. But those are my issues. Hawk thinks I'm beautiful, and he's happy just to hold me in his arms."

My phone buzzed in my pocketbook. We both looked down at my purse. I didn't need to take it out to know who was calling me. Again.

"Do you think this could be about something else?" Ellie hedged.

"You're asking if this is somehow my fault?"

"No, that's -"

"I gave him total control over me and he abused that power and fucked someone else. I'm tired of being fucked over. I'm just going to stay by myself."

I got up and marched away, leaving Ellie behind and my phone buried in my purse.

I stomped across the grounds, trying to drown

out Ellie's accusations. How could she think this was possibly my fault? I hadn't broken my promise to Owl. I'd given him more than I'd been prepared to give, and he took advantage. I was serious with what I'd said; I was done with men, done with dating. I obviously wasn't cut out for it.

I saw girls sitting under a tree, pretending to have a conversation with each other while looking at their phones and alternately looking around at the guys walking around the campus. They plumped up their breasts and flicked their hair any time one would come near.

I saw a couple embracing on a blanket. That look of love and devotion was in the girl's eyes. The guy looked up at me and winked.

I moved past it all without looking back. I made my way to my dorm. Only to find that what I was trying to get away from was there sitting on the floor outside my door.

TWENTY-ONE

Owl didn't get up when he saw me enter the hall. He just stared at me, his eyes drinking me in. He sat with his back against my dorm room door in dark jeans and a white, collared shirt. His legs were stretched out before him like he'd been there for quite a while.

"I don't want to talk to you," I said.

He looked down at his phone in his hand and nodded. Slowly, he brought his legs up under him and stood. He put his phone in his pocket. He brushed off the back of his pants and took a step.

I thought he was going to go. My heart screamed in my chest to stop him. It was the struggle of my life to stay still and silent.

"I'm going to..." He stopped, cleared his throat,

and then started again. "I would like to apologize for what happened the other day first, and then I'll go. I owe that much to you."

He stood there silently, waiting for my response. I wondered if I told him no, that I didn't want to hear any apology, to just go, would he?

His hands rested at his sides. I looked down at the floor instead of looking at the fingers that had been on that other woman. When I said nothing, I guess he took that as a sign to continue.

"I shouldn't have commanded you to come in the middle of the street like that. It was a violation and I'm sorry."

I glanced up at him. He stood there looking contrite and miserable. I heard my heart, as well as my resolve, crack at the sight of him. I had been so angry these last twenty-four hours I'd never thought about what he must be going through.

Wait, no. I didn't care what he was going through. He brought this on himself.

"That's it?" I asked. "That's all?"

Owl's handsome face crumbled in confusion. "Well, yes. I took advantage of something sacred between us by ordering you to come out in the wide-open while you were vulnerable. That was a betrayal of your trust. I promise you it will never happen again, and I hope you will forgive me. I'm willing to work to regain your trust."

I stared at him, trying to find his angle. Was he going to pretend the rest of it didn't happen? "What about the other part?"

He frowned, looking around the hall for a clue. "What other part?"

I dropped my bag on the floor and jerked my finger in the direction of his chest. "You cheated on me."

Owl held up his hands. It was a move of placation more than self-protection. When he spoke, he spoke very slowly as though I were a child just learning the English language. "Kira, aside from Ellie, who you said I could have sex with, I never fucked anyone after we committed to each other."

"Owl, I saw you with my own eyes. You had your hands on that woman."

"What woman?"

"In the garage."

He paused and tilted his head up as though to shake the memory lose. "Yeah, my hands. Not my mouth or my dick."

I stared at him. He truly didn't think he'd done anything wrong. I turned away from him, rubbing at the back of my neck.

Ellie was right. What I saw and what he did were two different things in each of our eyes. A hysterical laugh bubbled up and out of me.

"That's what we agreed on," he said. "Is touching like fucking to you?"

"Yes." The word came out on a choked laugh as I turned around to face him. "Yeah, Owl. Touching another woman's clit, even flicking at it, which sounds painful, is still fucking her in my book."

He approached me cautiously, his hands up where I could see them. "It's not to me," he said softly, gently. "I didn't understand that's what it meant to you. I was not trying to hurt you. I would never hurt you."

His voice was so coaxing. I wanted more than anything to believe him. To go into his arms and lay my head in that space in the middle of his chest that fit me so well. To listen as our heartbeats fell naturally into sync.

He hadn't meant to hurt me. It had been a mistake, a misunderstanding. He was owning up to it, not hiding from it. He saw that it hurt me and he was apologizing. He was promising not to do it again.

I believed him. I saw in his eyes that he was telling the truth. Owl always told the truth.

He stood before me, his arms outstretched, but he wasn't touching me. I watched his fingers jerk and tremble, as though reaching for me on their own accord, but he kept them away.

"If I had known it would've hurt you," he said, "I wouldn't have done it. Can we please go inside and talk about this?"

As soon as the door closed behind us, he pulled me into his arms. It felt amazingly good, like coming home. Not the home I'd just come from at my mother's. Not the home I'd made my dorm room into.

My body reacted to Owl like I was a part of him. He knew me so well after such a short time period. A large part of his intuition about me was because he paid attention to me. While he made love to me, his eyes were always wide open watching my reactions. But for someone who could read me so well, how could he not understand what his actions the other day would do to me?

"I just need to hold you for a minute," he whispered into my ear. "Where did you go? I couldn't find you. I was going out of my mind."

My fingers curled into his shoulder blades. I closed my eyes and buried my face in that special place for me in his chest. "I went home. To my mother's house," I clarified.

"Fuck," he held me tighter to him. "I don't even know where that is."

"Yeah, there's a lot we don't know about each other."

Owl pulled away, but didn't let me go. He stared into my face. His eyes roamed over my mouth, my cheeks, my eyes, all the way up to my hairline. "I want to change that, Kira. I'm not ready to lose you. I want this to work between us. We can have a closed relationship if that's what it'll take. No fucking, no touching, no body else."

My eyes took the same journey over the topography of his face. I searched his eyes for sincerity, his mouth for the truth, his cheeks for any blush of falsehood. But by the time I got to his hairline, I still wasn't sure. "Is that what you want?"

"I want you." He placed his lips on mine, softly, lightly, reverently.

My body instantly responded to him. It was like I'd been the dead walking for the past twenty-four hours, but I came alive in this moment just for him.

I pulled away. That was what I wanted, wasn't it? I should've felt certain, but I didn't.

"Kira?"

"It's me," I confessed. "It's not you."

"Baby, I don't understand."

Ellie was right. It had nothing to do with the sex. It was my insecurities that he would one day change his mind and leave me any way. I was so terrified of being alone that I didn't know how to actually be with someone.

"I can't," I said. "I can't do that to you. I can't do that to me. It's not what I need."

"Tell me what you need, Kira, and I'll give it to you."

I shook my head. "You can't. If we get back together this is just going to happen again because there are things I need to work on."

Owl reached for my hands and I gave them to him. "Let me help you."

I placed my hand on his heart and felt it beat strongly under my palm. "I rely too much on you for validation, Owl. I rely on you to tell me how to come, when to come."

"We don't have to do that any more."

"But I would still have to find my own voice, learn to hear my own desires. I gave you so much power over me because I didn't take it for myself. I need to be enough for me. I need to learn to please myself, to be by myself before I can be with anyone else. Otherwise we'll come right back to this point over and over again."

I watched the wheels turn in those dark eyes. I watched him search for a way through that could include him. I knew he arrived at the same conclusion as I did when he sighed and looked down at our entwined hands. The hurt look on his face almost made me change my mind.

He took a deep breath and let it out. "What do you need from me, Kira?"

I took a deep breath and nearly choked on the words I knew needed to be said. "I need you to give me some space."

Owl put his forehead against mine, pressing our temples together. His fingertips dug into my sides. He shook his head from left to right. Then he took a deep breath and sighed again. He pulled away from me with great reluctance. His jaw was tense, but it relaxed as he opened it.

"I love you," he said.

The words were whispered on a choked breath. Owl let out a huff of breath and said those three little words again, firmer this time.

My heart went into attack mode. It banged against my chest to get me back into his arms, but Owl held up his hands as though he knew what those words were doing to me.

"I'm not saying that to try and win you back.

Though you should be warned that I am going to try and win you back," he grinned. "I'm telling you this because I always tell you the truth, and you'd probably figure it out eventually."

He'd finally gotten something wrong about me. I would have never believed in a million years that he loved me. I couldn't have. Not in the state I'd lived most of my life in.

"I'm going to give you your space," he said. "But I'm probably gonna fuck up from time to time because... because I know that I want to be with you, and everything in me is telling me to stay and fight for you. But that's not going to work, is it?"

I shook my head no. I was shell-shocked that what I was pushing away from me was exactly what I would've killed for. It's what I snuck around and hacked phones and manipulated GPS's and blew guys for.

Owl wanted to stick around.

Owl wanted to fight for me.

Owl loved me.

And I was pushing him away.

He reached out his hand. He cupped my chin and rubbed my bottom lip. I leaned into his touch. I grabbed his wrist and held him there. He brushed his lips lightly against mine, and then he was gone.

TWENTY-TWO

"Hey, Kira."

I looked up from my packing box. "Hey, Ellie. What are you doing here?"

Ellie stood in the open doorway of my dorm room. Well, my former dorm room. It was dorm move out day tomorrow. It had been a week since I'd broken up with Owl in an attempt to find myself.

He'd kept his word, for the most part. He hadn't stopped by. He hadn't called. He had sent a few texts just to check in and make sure I was okay.

I hated to admit that I looked forward to those texts. I hadn't deleted a single one of them. I spent many nights in my bed by myself just looking at them, my finger hovering over the Talk button. The fact that I'd never once hit the Talk button this week was my only claim at progress in my great Self Improvement work.

Though, honestly, I wasn't exactly sure how I was supposed to go about strengthening myself into the independent, self-assured woman I wanted to be.

I had no interest in dating other guys. We'd come to the end of the school year, so I didn't have my studies to wrap myself up in. I had however landed a great summer job at the urban planning firm that I'd been part-timing for. I hoped that would keep me busy. But other than watching Oprah and Iyanla reruns, I didn't know what else to do with myself.

One thing that had changed? When I came home at night to an empty bed, I didn't lie down and fear the long night ahead. Every night since breaking up with Owl, I'd laid myself down along with the setting sun and I touched myself.

It took a couple of nights but I could bring myself to stronger and stronger orgasms. Only single orgasms, but they were satisfying enough to put me into a peaceful sleep where I'd dream about a dark-haired man with almond-shaped eyes.

Ellie stepped into the mess of flat cardboard and tape that was my former dorm room. "I came by to check in on you before summer starts. Since I've graduated, I won't be around campus any more. I wanted to see you before you went home for the summer."

"I'm not headed back home. I'm renting a one bedroom in the market district."

Her face brightened at the news. "So, you'll be here for the summer? Awesome! We can hang out."

I inhaled, bunching my shoulders and clutching my hands under my chin. "I don't think that's a good idea."

"Just because you and Owl broke up doesn't mean we can't be friends. The guys included. Crow and Eagle were just asking about you the other day."

Just the mention of Crow and Eagle made both my stomach and my clit grumble. "I don't know, sis?"

"You're not alone, Shakira. I know Owl is trying to give you the space you need, but there doesn't need to be space in our friendship, does there?"

I pulled my lower lip into my mouth. "I guess not. Maybe you can come over after I move in. It's going to take me forever to move these boxes."

"The guys will do that for you."

"I couldn't ask them to."

Ellie whipped out her phone and began texting. Not five seconds after she hit Send did her phone chime a response. "Eagle and Crow can be over here tonight. I'm sorry I can't stick around to help. Hawk and I are going away for the weekend. It's our first weekend alone together."

"Wow, that sounds awesome, sis."

Ellie nodded, her eyes going faraway into the future for her weekend alone with Hawk. My weekend would be spent alone, setting up an apartment that I would live in alone. The thing about self-improvement? There was just so much *self* in it. Maybe I was too hasty to turn away from Owl's offer to do this with me?

Take Ellie for example. She moved straight from her parents' house, to the college dorm, to her boyfriend's bed. She'd never taken a break to find herself and she seemed to be doing just fine.

But, that was her path. This was mine. Looking around my room I could admit to myself that I could use some help. Especially with the furniture that would be delivered later on tonight.

"I've gotta get going." Ellie headed towards the door.

"Hey, Ellie?"

"Yeah?" She turned back to me.

I walked over to her, reached out my arms, and gave her an awkward hug that progressively became warmer. "Thanks, sis."

Ellie pulled away with a smile. "That's what friends are for, Shakira."

Later that evening, I found myself inside another warm embrace.

"Kira, I missed you." Crow swooped me up into a bear hug. "Just cause Owl's a dick doesn't mean you get to write us all off."

"Owl's not a dick," I said. He wasn't. He'd told me exactly what he wanted and never wavered. He'd kept his word every step of the way. "I needed some time to work things out for myself."

"Well, I hope you figured it out," said Eagle as he filled the doorway of my old dorm room. "Cuz the dick insisted on coming with us."

I looked down the hall to see Owl lingering in the stairwell.

"Is it cool?" Eagle asked me. His body maneuvered to block my view of Owl, as though with one word from me and he'd escort Owl out of the building.

Eagle's gesture shocked me. I had assumed Owl, as his boy, would be a higher priority than me, someone he barely knew, and my needs. I looked over Eagle's shoulder.

Owl hung back making no attempt to advance. His eyes caught mine and held, doing that drinking me up glance he'd done the last time we were together. He may have insisted on coming, but he clearly wasn't trying to pressure me into anything I didn't want to do. He'd never tried to pressure me into anything I didn't want to do. None of these people had.

I rubbed Eagle on his bicep. "It's fine," I assured him. "The boxes are inside if you want to start loading them up."

Eagle placed a kiss on my brow and headed inside behind Crow. I turned back to Owl who still stood down the hallway.

"Hey," he called, not making a move towards me.

"Hey," I said. My eyes were now fastened on him, drinking him in. He wore faded jeans and a t-shirt. He'd come ready to work, ready to help me make my move. But he hung back prepared to get lost if I turned him away.

"Come here," I said.

Owl made his way towards me. I watched his powerful body move lithely. I had to swallow to keep down my desire to run and leap into his arms. That wouldn't be a very independent thing to do.

"I changed my mind," he said when he got to me. "I know you need your space, and I'm willing to give that to you. But it shouldn't mean I can't be in your life. Not as your boyfriend or your lover. But as something, Kira. Your friend maybe? You don't have to be alone as you figure these things out. You're important to me. I don't want our entire relationship to end because of sexual issues. If after you have your reflection time, you take stock and believe that I'm of no value to you-"

"I've taken stock," I said. "You've always gone out of your way to earn my trust. You've always been honest with me. And you've always shown me respect. You're of great value to me, Owl."

He smiled, but he made no move to close the distance between us. Eagle came out of the door and between us with boxes in hand.

"If the *After School Special* is over," said Eagle to Owl, "we could use a hand."

Owl grinned at me over top of the boxes. Once Eagle cleared the door, he went inside and loaded up on boxes alongside Crow. They wouldn't let me carry any loads. They asked what needed to go and where, and they took care of the rest.

TWENTY-THREE

"The picture's askew," I told Crow. "Move it a little to the left."

We were standing in the living room of my new apartment. All the boxes were inside. All the furniture unloaded and put together.

"Here, I'll get it." Owl took the frame out of Crow's hand and aligned it perfectly on the first try.

"We brought you a lasagna," said Crow. He pulled a dish out of his bag.

"You didn't have to do that," I said.

"I was raised with manners. Someone moves into a new home, you bring a housewarming gift." Crow went over to the fridge and popped it on one of the empty shelves.

"We're having a party in a couple nights," said Eagle. "We'd love to see you there."

I turned my head away from Owl's view as I contemplated the invitation. "I don't know if I'm ready for that?"

"Well, we can always have a private party." Crow came up and wrapped his arms around me. "You shouldn't deny yourself, Kira. Or us. I miss those pretty, Hershey Kisses."

Crow nuzzled the side of my neck. It was a good thing he'd wrapped his arms around my waist because my knees buckled on impact. Crow licked the side of my neck as his hand snaked under my shirt. I closed my eyes and let my head roll back into his shoulder.

"Can I have a taste, Kira?"

I opened my eyes to Eagle's voice. But my vision slid past Eagle's large frame and landed on Owl.

Owl stood in the kitchen. A pass through window divided him from us. He made no move to come nearer to the action. He'd been keeping his distance from me all evening long. No accidental brushes or touches. He was going out of his way to keep space between us.

I found it irritating.

Crow's hands, which were edging the under-wire of my bra, felt so good I moaned.

Owl's hands clenched onto the edge of the kitchen counter. He backed himself up into the corner as though he were giving me more space. Or maybe giving himself the space he needed to stay away from me and out of this impending ménage.

I turned my back to Owl. I unbuttoned my shirt. Crow bent down and took my breast into his mouth; bra, lace, and all. I closed my eyes. This is exactly what I had been missing in this whole self-improvement work. I'd been denying this attention to myself; this attention that had been the only thing to set me free and flying into the air.

Eagle's hands ran up my thigh. He hoisted me up onto my new four-person dining room table. He pulled up a chair and sat between my thighs. I couldn't see Owl, but I knew he was there. I knew he was watching as Eagle relieved me of my panties and made a dessert of my pussy.

Eagle made slow circles around my pussy while Crow played with my nipples. Eagle inserted two fingers inside my pussy as he continued stroking my flesh with his tongue. I arched my body back, which pushed my breasts further into Crow's mouth.

Already, I was trembling, my body ascending

that cliff that led to oblivion. My toe was already at the edge in the blink of an eye. And then I realized it.

I could come right here and now. My body was primed for it. All it would take would be for me to let go and take the dive.

I opened my eyes and found Owl. He stood still, tucked away in the corner of the kitchen, eyes rapt on me. He said nothing. He didn't even give me a cheeky grin. He just watched me. I could tell by the look in his eyes he knew I was close to coming, but he gave me no commands. He kept his distance as promised.

In that moment, I decided to keep hold of my orgasm. Not because I didn't want to share it with the men who were pleasuring me. I kept it in because I wanted them to take me higher. I was certain Owl read my thoughts because I spied the slightest uptick of his mouth.

I turned away from Owl and laid my body down on the table. My new position pushed my hips closer into Eagle's sweet tongue. I turned my head and motioned for Crow to give me his dick.

Crow fucked into my mouth while he continued to play with my nipples. My legs were trembling under Eagle's tongue and Crow's fingers. But it wasn't torture. I danced on that cliff. I wanted the song of our pleasure to never end.

Eagle lifted me up and brought me to lean over the table. He spread my legs wide leaving my ass in the air. From somewhere he produced a condom and a packet of lube. Excitement made my ass cheeks clench when I realized where we were going with this. I remembered Eagle telling me I would come when he got a hold of my ass.

My eyes caught ahold of Owl still standing sentry in the corner of the kitchen. It was clear he read the excitement on my face. His eyes glazed over as they ran over my body from my dangling breasts to my ass, which was high in the air waiting for another man to claim it.

There was no jealousy in Owl's eyes. I didn't expect there to be. Not even now when we were apart. Owl had always taken joy in my pleasure whether it was at his hand, my own, or someone else's. Now, I wanted to share this with him. My eyes stayed on Owl as Eagle rubbed the oil over my anus.

Eagle took me slowly. He pushed the head of his cock in past that little ring of fire. Once he was clear, and I let go of the tension, he began slow, shallow thrusts to get me used to his girth.

I knew Eagle and Crow. I trusted them. I knew they wanted nothing more than to get me off and get off themselves in the process. I arched back into Eagle, letting him know I could take more, that I wanted to take more.

Eagle went a little deeper, a little faster. His motions were hypnotic, awakening pleasure centers in me that I didn't know were back there.

Crow took a seat on the table and offered me his dick. I took it gladly, needing an outlet for so much pleasure building in my body. I slurped over Crow's dick as Eagle fucked my ass.

When I could keep my eyes open for longer than a few seconds, I'd find Owl. He was no longer gripping the edge of the kitchen counter. He leaned against the pass through window that looked out on the dining area. His chin rested in his hand, his eyes full of a love I couldn't pretend I didn't see.

Eagle's thrusts sped up. The pleasure went from dancing on the cliff, to taking a running leap. My body went from zero to one hundred and an orgasm from a place I'd never come before took over. I'd never worked the muscles in my ass, so I had no control over them.

I contracted around Eagle's thick cock, which continued to thrust and hit those nerves deep inside of me. I had to let go of Crow's cock or risk clamping down on him. I howled my pleasure, loud enough that I'm sure my new neighbors knew that I'd arrived. And still Eagle didn't stop thrusting.

The orgasm raged on and on until I had to lurch my body off his dick for a chance to take a breath. My lungs had constricted from panting so much for so long. Eagle gave me a moment to collect myself. But only a moment.

In that moment, Crow suited up and climbed beneath me. My clit lurched again as it anticipated what they were about to do to me. I looked up and found Owl leaning over the divide between the kitchen and dining room table. His eyebrow arched to make sure I was good with this. I grinned back at him. He chuckled, crossed his arms over his chest, and rested his head on his forearm to watch the show.

They settled me over Crow's hips. Crow entered me first. He slid in like butter onto the nooks and crannies of my English Muffin. Eagle was a different story. He entered me slowly from behind as Crow played with my nipples to distract me from the increasingly tight fit. And then they began to move.

One and then the other. Crow pumped into my pussy. Eagle thrust deep into my ass. I lost track of everything outside of the channels of my ass and vagina. Even those two places I couldn't focus on at the same time. I reveled in the familiar fullness of my vaginal walls being stretched. Then I'd turn and marvel at the rousing nerves in my ass.

They pumped faster, still alternating. Just as an orgasm would build in my pussy, Crow would withdraw and Eagle would spark something by filling my ass. The two orgasms were coming from different places inside of me, both of which were pulling for my attention. It was like having my feet on different sides of a steep hill. I could topple over either side.

Instead of one or the other, I fell from both at the same time. My pussy and ass clenched simultaneously. The intense pleasure brought tears to my eyes and sobs to my mouth.

From somewhere in the distance, I heard the sound of deep, animalistic groans. Crow and Eagle each came as they both pushed inside me, stretching me to capacity as my body held all three of us in a death grip.

Nothing much made sense after that. I remembered the cold of the wooden table on my bare ass. I remembered a light kiss on one of my nipples. I remembered the sound of Eagle's voice telling me not to be a stranger. I caught a flash of my red underwear as it disappeared into a back pants pocket. I heard the front door click shut. My eyes finally opened when I felt the warm water surrounding my body.

"Hey," Owl said as he supported me in the tub.

"Hey," I smiled and closed my eyes, allowing him to care for me in the aftermath of that mind-shattering orgasm.

TWENTY-FOUR

Owl didn't touch me sexually while he sponged me down. His attention was clearly fixed on getting me dry when he toweled me off. He lifted me into his arms and carried me into my bedroom.

It would've been romantic if he'd been gazing into my eyes. But he didn't do that. His eyes were on the path before us as he negotiated the boxes and debris from the unpacking. Once in my bedroom, he slid back the covers I'd put on a couple of hours ago.

"Do you want me to get you a t-shirt or underwear to sleep in?" he asked.

I shook my head as I looked at him standing above me. I didn't need any underwear. What I really wanted was for him to climb in next to me and hold me through the first night in this strange bed, in this new room.

"You need anything else, Kira?" His dark eyes studied me, seeing right through me.

My eyes fixed on his chest. I could clearly make out his pecs beneath his t-shirt. I spied that space in between where I used to lay my head after he'd fuck me. "No, I think I'm good."

"Okay," he paused, uncertain. "I brought this for you."

He reached into his back pocket and handed me what looked to be a homemade craft. It was a piece of cloth with intricate markings on it.

"It's called an *Omamori*."

"*Omamori*," I parroted.

He sat down on the edge of the bed next to me. "It's a talisman, sort of like a Native American dreamcatcher. It will protect you in the night when you sleep by yourself. But it's also a…" He struggled for the translation from Japanese to English culture. "A well-wish. Because that's what I want for you; to be happy and well."

Owl ran his hand lightly across my temple. Inside, I felt my heart weeping tears.

"Call me if you need anything, even if you just

want to talk. I want you to know that I'm here for you. Okay?"

I nodded.

He rose from beside me on the bed. I looked down at the impression he'd made in the new mattress.

"Owl?"

He stopped and turned.

But I couldn't make my mouth work. I had taken this great big stand about needing space, about being on my own, about figuring out what I wanted. When the truth was, what I wanted was standing before me waiting patiently to be invited back into my life.

"It's kind of late," Owl said. "Would you mind if I stayed until morning? Just this night, your first night. I'd just hold you. We don't need to do anything else."

"I don't want to do anything else," I said. "I mean, I would like to be held. It's exactly what I was wishing for."

Owl grinned. He kicked off his shoes and came back to the bed. I held open the covers for him, flashing my naked body, but he shook his head.

"That's dangerous territory. I'm not a saint, Kira."

He tucked me back under the covers and lay on

top of the sheets. He pulled me into him, right into that space in his chest where I fit perfectly. In a matter of minutes, I was asleep.

When I opened my eyes next, the sun's rays were still tucked into the horizon. I shifted to find Owl wide-awake, staring down at me.

"Hey," I said.

"Hey," he mimicked. "Did you need me to go now?"

"Go?"

"The last thing I want to do is wear out my welcome, Kira."

I shook my head from side-to-side on the pillow-case. "You don't have to go. I'm comfortable."

"Me, too."

I slid my covered leg between his and met his morning wood against my thigh.

"I said that I would keep my distance," Owl grinned. "He has a mind of his own."

I laughed putting my head back in that space between his pecs, the space that seemed to mold around my head. "Owl?"

"Mmm?"

"I'm still trying to figure things out with myself, with us, with others. But there's one thing I know for sure." I reached out and put my hand on his dick. "I like being close to him."

Owl's jaw tensed as I touched him. He searched my eyes for something. I wasn't sure what? He leaned in, and then stopped himself. Finally, he just asked.

"Can I kiss you?"

I smiled. "Of cou-"

His lips crashed into mine. His hands went into my hair, clasping me to him. My instinct was to go slack in his arms, to let him have his way with me. But I shoved that idea by the wayside. I clutched back at him, giving as good as I got. He pulled away, grinning down at me, looking at me in a new light as the sun rose.

"Are you sore?" he asked.

I set my mouth to say no, but felt the twinge as I clenched my thighs from the want of him.

"Lay back, baby. Let me take care of you." Owl stood, sweeping the sheet off my body. He disappeared into the bathroom and reemerged with a travel-sized tube of baby oil in his hand. Then he undressed quickly and climbed back on the bed.

He came between my legs. I opened my thighs for him. I knew where this was going.

He began the same sensual massage he'd given

Ellie. Only he rubbed his hands all over my body. My shoulders, my back, my breasts, the balls of my feet, between each toe, then up and between each finger, all before he arrived at my core.

We breathed in unison as he traced circles around my pubic bone. I arched into his touch as he rubbed first my right and then my left labia. That tapping thing he did with the tips of his fingers; that made me want to grab his dick and shove it inside of me right now. As though he read my mind, he finally took his dick and brought it to my core.

We both sighed as he entered me. He slid into what we both knew was his home after he'd cleaned up the beautiful mess our guests had made of me. He didn't thrust right away, and I was glad for it. I needed a moment to soak him in. It was the first time I'd felt whole in days.

I knew I still had work to do on myself. I wasn't yet the woman I was striving to be. I knew that if Owl were to leave me tomorrow, I would have a really hard time with it. I knew that I still had trust and abandonment issues, not just when it came to my man, but to my friends.

I was not yet wholly who I wanted to be. But I knew in this moment of deep penetration that I would get there following an easier path if this man and his crew of friends were by my side.

"Is it okay to say I love you?" he asked me while our bodies were one. "Because that's what I'm feeling right now."

"I feel it too, Owl."

He smiled down at me. "I'm not going to take advantage of that. I know you still need your space to find yourself. But I am going to fuck you so hard right now you're going to forget who you are."

I laughed, but my laughter was short lived as he made good on his promise. He fucked me so hard that my teeth chattered. He fucked me so hard that my toes curled into my heels. He fucked me so hard that I felt it in my ass.

An orgasm built deep inside of me, but as it came to the top of the mountain it looked from me to him, uncertain who it would listen to for permission to fly. Owl kept his mouth shut as he continued to pummel into me. I closed my eyes, took a deep breath, and let myself go.

As I climaxed, I felt him falling down with me. Our hands entwined, our hearts beat in sync. We crashed into each other and we didn't let go.

The sun was high when we finally crawled out

of the bed and got dressed. At the door, Owl pulled me into an embrace.

"I'm not putting any restraints or constraints on you, Kira. Open or closed, it doesn't make a difference. I just want to love you, baby."

I cuddled into the spot in his chest that was mine and heard in his heartbeat the truth of his words.

"I know it's going to take time to rebuild the trust we had," he continued. "But I want you to know that I respect you and will respect your boundaries. If you want to explore other relationships, I will support you -if you want me there. Or I will stay out of your way if you need the space to do it on your own. Just know that at the end of the day, I want the opportunity to be the one who holds you."

It was all I'd ever wanted in a relationship. He'd wrapped it in a neat little bow, a bow without any knots or passcodes, and handed it to me. I reached over into a side table and withdrew my spare key. I placed it in Owl's hands.

He looked down at the key with a raised eyebrow. "This is a lot of power you're placing in my hands."

I smiled, planting a kiss on his cheek. "I trust you to not over step your boundaries."

Owl jingled the solo key on the ring. "Maybe I

can come back tonight?"

I leaned against the doorjamb and nodded, not even bothering to play a game of coyness. Because the truth was, he was offering me exactly what I wanted. "Maybe I'll come to your crew's party."

He planted a chaste kiss on my brow. "If you do, I'll be ready when you come for me, Kira."

Owl turned and walked down the hall. Not until he was out of sight and the door was closed, did I allow myself to sink down to the ground as the orgasm from his words wracked through my body.

The story is not over!

Crow is about to fall hard for a romance author. She'll need his help to write the steamy bits.
Problem is, she's never done the steamy bits.
Lucky for her, Crow's happy to be her hero and "tweak" her body as well as her words!

Read Dangerous Curves Ahead, Book 3 in the Watchers Crew series.

Turn the page to check out the start of their happily ever after...

DANGEROUS CURVES AHEAD SNEAK PEEK!

Chapter One

THE TAPPING of raindrops on the window was intermittent; sometimes a steady pitter-patter, then in the next minute, a reluctant deluge. The thick droplets dried up immediately after impact when they hit the glass pane. The disappearing act was likely due to the brilliant sun shining above.

It was the kind of day my grandfather would've called God weeping for mankind. It was the kind of day my father would've called God pissing on mankind. In my opinion it was a great day.

The winter was over. I was out of the knits and sweaters that added bulk to my curvy frame. Today,

I was in one of my favorite sundresses. Sundresses allowed me to come out of my shell and show off my best assets; my calves and shoulders. Though most of the time, the male gaze stayed focused on the double D's on my chest.

I sat in a pretty floral dress, my wedged heels crossed at my ankles. My toenails were done in a fun design that matched my fingernails, which also matched the ribbon I'd tied in my hair, which also complimented the floral earrings dangling from my lobes. Because I was never comfortable showing too much skin, I may have been prone to over-accessorizing.

I wasn't a flashy person. Though I did often use my clothing to reflect my mood. And today, I felt a rainbow of optimism on the horizon.

Also on the horizon, across the street in an office building, I spied a man in a business suit and a woman in a blouse and skirt making out. The man had the woman pressed up against the closed door. My eyes widened as his hands went up her shirt.

From this distance, I saw the divot of her belly button. I'd seen any number of belly buttons in my lifetime; on the beach, in the girl's locker room, walking down the street on a Saturday night. But in this context, there was something wicked about it.

I wasn't wicked. I was a good girl. But I couldn't look away.

The man's palm traveled under her blouse up higher and higher on her torso. My eyes kept in step with his fingers. My hand clutched at my chest at the sight of her bra; lacy and fire-engine red. He pulled the bra cup down and exposed her nipple. The contrast to the red lace and the pink areola was stark.

A crack of thunder split the air, darkening the skies and scattering the raindrops. The two broke apart. They looked out the window, up at the darkening sky. At the same time, I jumped in my seat. I averted my gaze, doubtful they saw me.

I pressed a hand to my cheeks to feel them flaming. Then reached down to finger the rosary beads at my heart. The texture of the beads calmed me. When I looked up, the couple was gone. The office was empty.

I took a deep breath and turned from the window. Glancing up at the utilitarian wall clock, I noted that my appointment should've started fifteen minutes ago.

My fifth book in Hera Publishing's inspirational romance line had just reached into the top 10,000 on Amazon. There were over a million books available for sale at the online retailer. That was a big deal for an inspirational author like me who ended each book with the hero and heroine approaching first base. It proved that readers wanted more of my self-assured heroines who met their heroes inside church groups instead of the stepbrother down the hall or the werewolf who threw her over his shoulder.

My first series, *Righteous Calling*, was comprised of twenty-something, career women who returned to their small towns, and then back to their roots in church, to reconnect with their Creator. Along the way, they each found love amidst the pews. I sat in my editor's office waiting to pitch my next series.

The series I hoped to write next was called *Tender Kisses*. For this series, I planned to go with the tide of the market and write new adult characters. These love stories would be about Christians meeting at Bible college. I was also debating pitching a future series called *Love's Calling* about missionaries finding romance while abroad.

I wasn't making a killing selling sweet romances, but they paid the bills. It was enough so that I didn't have to rely on my parents for money. My mother would love nothing more than to have me back home. That was the last thing I wanted; being the buffer in my parents' marriage. *Til death do us part* was less a vow and more a threat in my parents' case.

The pitter-patter of the rain died down, and I heard the striking of heels across the floor. Moira Young walked into her office in fire-red stilettos and a black designer pantsuit that fit her size six waist like a glove. Her face looked professionally made up as though she'd walked off a high-fashion shoot. Her lip-gloss was perfect for her dark skin tone. She could've been Tyra Banks's more attractive sister. Sitting in my flower dress and hair bows, I felt like anything but *America's Next Top Model*.

I sucked in my size twelve gut which caused my double D's to rise. I'd managed eyeliner and gloss, but that was the extent of my makeup collection. Most of my advance and royalties went to my closet, which I used to hide my chubby flaws.

Moira had taken over the publishing house after my third book had been published. My last editor had left, gone off to a big New York publishing house. She'd taken a few authors with her. I hadn't been included.

That was fine. I was loyal to Hera Publishing. This company had given me my first break. I planned to stay with them for the long haul.

"All right, Mary Kate."

I forced a smile. I hated when people truncated my name. But I wanted to start this meeting off on a positive note.

Moira looked up at me with a thousand-watt smile that didn't reach her smoke-lined eyes.

"I'm excited to talk about your future with the company," she said in an even tone.

Her even tone didn't alarm me. Moira never spoke in exclamation points. Only periods and semi-colons.

I, on the other hand, was prone to exclaim. "I'm excited, too!"

"We're making some changes," Moira continued, glazing over my expression. "You're a valued author for Hera Publishing. You have a loyal, but small following."

My following wasn't small. Had she not read the latest author report? I wasn't exactly one in a million, but 10,000 wasn't half bad.

"I think it could be bigger," Moira said. "We want to take you in a new direction."

Perfect. I opened my mouth to pitch my *Tender Kisses* and *Love's Calling* series.

Before I could, Moira continued. "We want you to add steam."

Steam? As in steam punk? I had no clue about that genre. It also had no place in inspirational and sweet romance. It was more in the realm of science fiction and fantasy romance.

When Moira came onboard, Hera introduced a few new lines. The Athena line, for paranormal, science fiction, and fantasy romance. The Dione line, for contemporary. And the Aphrodite line, for erotica. With my current sales, I felt fairly secure that my career would continue at the Demeter line, for the sweeter side of romance. Was she asking me to write for the Athena line?

"Many Christian authors, inspirational authors, and sweet authors are opening the doors during their love scenes," Moira said. "There's even Amish erotica."

So I'd heard. I wasn't Amish. I'd been raised in a traditional Christian household. The kind where the parents stop going to church after the kids outgrew their fancy Easter clothes.

"Your readers are buying it," Moira said.

I frowned, having lost the train of conversation. "It?"

Moira paused and blinked at me as though she remembered I was there while she gave her monologue. "Sex. Your readers are buying books with sex in them."

I wanted to disagree. I wanted to insist that my readers were girls just like me. Good girls, who sat with their legs crossed, and went to church every Sunday.

Well, I didn't go to church every Sunday. In fact, I hadn't been since... last Easter? I think?

"If you want to keep writing for us, Mary Kate, you're going to have to pop your heroines' cherries."

This time it was me who paused and blinked. I shook my head like I used to shake the bunny ear antennas on my grandparents' old television. There had to be something wrong with the reception.

"You can keep the story lines in your wheel house," Moira said. "I'd love to see a good girl go on a sexual journey of discovery with a bad boy in need of redemption. I'll need to see an outline and the first three chapters by the end of the month."

An outline? I hadn't been required to submit an outline since my first book. Not only was I being asked to write something completely out of my depth, I was being treated like a new author.

"And what if I don't want to add steam or open doors in my stories?" I asked.

Moira frowned as though she hadn't considered

the query. "You can always buy out your existing contract. But you still owe us two more books."

I didn't have the money lying around to buy out of two books. I was budgeted down to the penny. I opened my mouth to bargain, but Moira's phone rang. She picked up the receiver. I was effectively dismissed.

I rose, preparing to leave the office. I cast a glance out the window. On the bright side, the sky had cleared, taking the rain away. Off in the distance, I spied the multicolored stripes of a rainbow. I was just on the wrong end of the arch.

CHAPTER Two

BY THE TIME I stepped out of Hera Publishing's office, the rainbow showed bright across the sky. Unfortunately, it did not brighten my mood. I walked over to my car; a Chevy Buick. Not one of the newer models in the young hipster commercials. It was a 1970's model. I'd gotten it from my grandfather. He'd named the car Lucille because she had the devil in her.

I sat back in Lucille's plush seat and closed my eyes. What was I going to do? It's not like I was a literary author out for awards for my craft.

I wrote romance novels.

A lot of people looked down on the genre. In my four years of writing in the industry, I'd met so many women who were feeding their families with the money they garnered from writing what the general public called bodice rippers, chick lit, and mommy porn.

I didn't turn my nose up at steamy romance. It just wasn't my thing. But it would have to become my thing if I wanted to keep making a living.

So, what were my options?

I could quit. Take my work to another publisher. Hope that my audience followed me. But I could be sued for breach because I owed the publisher more books.

Or, I could give them what they wanted. Sex.

I turned the ignition over. Lucille groaned, shuddered, and stalled.

Two race cars sped down the street, engines roaring, exhaust polluting the air. It was an increasing problem in the city, just like teenage pregnancy in high schools, the spread of STDs in elder communities, and the rate of divorce in mature communities. People were all moving too fast.

Twenty minutes later, I pulled up to my parents' pristine house. The lawn was recently manicured. The shutters had a fresh coat of paint. There were bright flowers blooming in the window box.

Inside, my sister's kids were wreaking havoc in the family room. Louisa Mae had four children under the age of six. She greeted me belly first with number five. Her thick brown tresses were coiled in an elaborate knot on top her head, not a hair out of place. Eye shadow highlighted her green eyes, and a thin sheen of lip-gloss accented her full lips.

We had the exact same facial features, but that's where it ended. Even though she was five months pregnant, she carried her baby weight well. Her figure still held its hourglass. Any weight she'd gained belonged to the baby in her belly and didn't dare touch anywhere else on her body.

"You're late," Louisa Mae said. "I've been playing referee with the parents for the last hour."

"Mommy," said one of her boys. Honestly, I couldn't tell if he was Walter or Brandon. They looked exactly alike except for an inch or two. "He hit me!"

"Go give him a hug and show him that in this family we love," was my sister's response.

The kid pouted off, unsatisfied. I doubted a hug was on the horizon.

"Are they fighting?" I said, indicating my head towards the kitchen where I saw my mom moving about.

"You know they never fight. They barely talk," said my sister. "It's a cold front."

I looked around the living room. "Where's your husband?"

"Business trip." Louisa Mae struggled with a diaper bag. There were bags under her eyes that would never blend into her eye shadow. "He just got a new account and has to be available to his clients at all times."

Charles, Louisa Mae's husband, was some corporate bigwig. I wasn't sure exactly what he did? Mainly because I had never had a full conversation with the man in the seven years he'd been my brother-in-law. He wasn't around the family much, but he was always available to his clients.

My two-year-old niece, who was dressed as a pink fairy with wings, was throwing a tantrum over her cartoon program ending. Louisa Mae tried to explain that mommies couldn't make the television network play the episode again. The two eldest boys weren't hugging; they were shoving at each other behind their mother's back. The one-year-old sat quietly on the sofa watching it all go down. I couldn't tell if he was taking notes or wishing he were somewhere else.

My sister found another program for the fairy princess and then separated the two eldest boys. "What took you so long to get here?" she said to me.

"Meeting at my publisher's," I said from my post in the doorway. "My editor wanted to discuss some upcoming projects."

My sister frowned. "You're still writing those smutty stories?"

I felt like throwing a tantrum myself. Maybe that would get my sister to change the channel away from this repeated argument. "They want to take my books in a new direction. They really believe in my talent."

It wasn't exactly a lie. Moira said she believed in my talent. She just wanted me to take my talent in an area where I was uncomfortable treading.

"I don't know how you'll ever find a husband with a hobby like that," Louisa Mae said as she arched her back with a grimace. "Aren't most romance writers women? Plus you're going to keep packing it on if you sit around all day typing on keyboards. You might as well become a secretary. At least that way you could try to snag your boss or a junior executive."

Louisa Mae walked into the fray of her children, who were now bickering over the remote control, before I could mount a counteroffensive. The only reason my sister went to college was to get her MRS degree. When that didn't work, she got a job as an Executive Assistant and that's where she met Charles Rasmussen. There was already a Mrs. Rasmussen, but Charles had insisted they were separated. Luckily, he was divorced before Walter, or was it Brandon, had been born. But it wasn't something we talked about.

I left my sister to her family and turned to the matriarch of our own.

"Ah, there you are, Mary Katherine."

Pricilla Elizabeth Wallace straightened, pulling a roast out of the oven. She was dressed in a tailored skirt and blouse, looking every bit the Economics Professor she was. My mother was in her early fifties, but she could easily be mistaken for her late thirties. When we were out together, which wasn't often, we were mistaken for sisters.

"How was your writing club meeting?"

"It was fine, mom. Thanks for asking." I didn't bother to correct her. It was fruitless.

Because our mother was a professor, we always had the expectation of getting higher education degrees. My sister studied Art History, so she could be witty at company parties. I'd minored in Literature and majored in Secondary Education my first year in college.

The Education degree wasn't my idea. It was the only way my mother would pay for such a frivolous minor. She wanted to be sure I had an actual career opportunity on the horizon if my first intention wasn't to find a husband to support me. That career opportunity was teaching. I'd submitted my sweet romance stories in my sophomore year. By my junior year, I had enough money from my first advance to pay for the extra credits for a double major.

My mother placed the roast on the stovetop. She turned and frowned. "Oh Mary Katherine, I wish you'd dressed for dinner."

I looked down at myself. My floral sundress was fine for a business meeting. I thought it was all right for a family dinner. That is, if this was just a family dinner.

"Why?" I looked down the hallway to the front door. "It's just us, right?"

Mom didn't meet my eyes "Where's your father? I asked him to bring in an extra chair. I swear the man is useless. I even wrote it down for him."

"Mom? Why would we need an extra chair if it's just us four at the adult table?"

"And I'm sure you'll only want one helping of the roast." My mother glanced at my Spanx-addled midsection, pretending not to hear me.

I knew she was pretending because she had the same crinkle in her eye she got when my father spoke to her.

"Kurt," she called.

"You don't have to yell, Priscilla." My dad entered the kitchen. Unlike my mother, my father looked his age. The years hadn't been kind to him and he had developed a bit of a beer belly along with a streak of gray in his brown hair. But he was still very handsome.

"I'm right here," he said.

"You weren't right here," insisted my mother. "That's why I had to yell. You didn't bring the extra chair."

"Extra chair for who?" My dad turned and saw me. His face lit up as though he saw a small spot of shade in the glaring sun. "Hello, Mary Katherine."

Dad leaned in and bussed me on the cheek.

Mixed in with his cologne was a floral scent I knew wasn't my mother's brand of perfume. Pulling away, I caught a shade of lipstick on his collar that didn't match my mother's skin tone.

"Hey, Daddy." I smiled and kept my mouth shut. It wasn't something we talked about.

My father had been out of work for two years now. Before that my mom had quickly surpassed him as breadwinner. Before I went to college, I'd noticed that the extra set of guest sheets were often missing from the linen closet. I once found them in my sister's old room. I don't know the last time my parents slept in the same bedroom. Or the last time they'd shown any affection towards each other. My writing got me out of the house and out from under my mom's thumb. Dad wasn't so lucky.

"Kurt, will you please get an extra chair?" My mother's tone was a pitch perfect match to my sister's who I could hear scolding one of the boys in the other room.

My father scowled, but turned and did as he was told.

"Who's coming to dinner, Mom?"

"Did I not tell you? The local high school is looking for an English teacher?"

"I met the principal at the school board meeting," said my sister coming into the kitchen. "He's young and handsome."

"And single," said my mom.

Dad came back into the kitchen with the extra chair.

My mother pointed to indicate where my father should set the chair; right next to my usual spot at the dinner table. "So when he gets here, Mary Katherine, don't talk about those little romance stories you write. We wouldn't want him to think you'd be teaching the kids trashy writing."

I stared at the chair that my father unfolded and placed next to my spot. I looked over at my mother, who was carving a thin slice of roast that had my name on it. I glanced at my sister who rubbed her belly absentmindedly with her left hand until her wedding band snagged the fabric of her dress. I looked back at my father who glared at my mother behind her back as he shoved the guest chair up to the table.

I saw the bars at the back of the chair; the unbendable, cold, steel bars. My feet moved towards the front door of their own accord. "I can't stay."

"But it's family night," said my dad. His hand reached out toward me as though I were a puffy cloud taking away his moment in the shade.

"I have a deadline for one of those trashy stories," I said. "It's on my brain and since Mom doesn't want me to talk about it in front of your guest..."

I didn't bother to finish the sentence. I made a beeline for the front door. Then I ran until I got to Lucille. She started on the first try. We tore out of there -speed limit be damned. When I got home, I knew my only choice would be to open up some doors and let out some steam.

CHAPTER Three

A FEW DAYS LATER, my hands still shook from signing the new publishing contract. I stood to make more money for the first steamy book than I made in my last three, sweet books combined. I'd spent the last few days researching the erotic romance industry. A lot of paperback books were tossed across my apartment in disgust. I couldn't believe that modern, thinking, autonomous women were truly into these things.

Billionaires.   Stepbrothers.   Pseudo-incest. Spanking?

I was trying to get away from my family. Not pull them into my bedroom!

By the end of the week, I still had no clue how I would turn my sweet, virginal heroines into wanton, sexpots that shook their naughty booties at their new daddies or brothers by marriage.

I was already on plan D when I pulled up to a storefront on the other side of town. It did not look like a sex shop. It looked like a boutique sandwiched between a beauty supply store and an electronics store. Across the street was a Babies R Us.

I'd been sitting in my car watching people go in and out of the front doors of Adonis' Novelties. They were a mixed crowd. Mostly middle-aged couples or women of an undeterminable age. It couldn't have been a den of heathens if mature people went in. I just hadn't seen anyone come back out yet.

The website for Adonis' Novelties said they held classes and sold educational and sexual health products. That's why I was here.

I couldn't get past the first few chapters of the best-selling, steamy romance books. I'd tried watching porn online and never got past the first five minutes of any scene. It was so clear that the women in these grainy videos were 'working' and not enjoying the benefits. They kept swiping their hair out of the way of the camera lens. Their heavily made-up faces kept checking for the placement of the camera, paying more attention to it than their coworkers. And their moaning and dirty talking had me hitting the mute button. I didn't know what an orgasm felt like, having never had one myself, but it was clear that their show of passion was all faked.

So, I was here at this adult boutique shop that promised art porn for women by women. I just needed to go in there and get what I needed in order to do my job and keep my independent lifestyle.

I got out of the comfort of Lucille and crossed the parking lot. No sooner did I step onto the side-walk did two cars zoom up, motors growling. Wheels screeched in protest and smoke rose from beneath the tires. The drivers did a turn I'd only seen in the movies and slid perfectly into the parking lines, landing side by side.

Inside the vehicles, two young men laughed as they shouted at each other through open windows. In the car closer to me was a black man with dark shades that hid his eyes. Even with the shades, I could tell he was looking at me. Through to his passenger window, I saw a blond man. He wore no sunglasses and his smiling, blue eyes pierced my soul. The mischief in them made a giggle bubble in my chest. The heat in them had me pressing my thighs together and ducking my head as my cheeks prepared to blush.

The blond cut his engine and got out. The dark-skinned man held up his middle finger. The blond continued laughing as he crossed the street.

The dark-skinned man turned his gaze back to me. His head dipped, allowing me to see his eyes behind the shades. He scanned my body with a curl to his lip that made me gulp. Men rarely looked at me like that. I felt the heat pouring off of him as he sucked in his lower lip. He dipped his shades down lower, so I saw the intention in his eyes. He winked at me before pulling off in a roar of engines.

When I looked up, the blond was checking me out. His eyes fastened to my breasts. I crossed my arms over my chest. That's when he met my eyes. His were unapologetic and crystal blue. Fathomless blue, like seeing down into the ocean. Only it went on forever and ever.

"Are you headed in?"

I gasped in a lungful of air as his voice brought me back to the surface. I looked at the storefront door. My cheeks blazed red. My mouth wouldn't work to deny my intended destination.

He opened the door for me. Then, to my horror, he followed me inside. He was obviously a creep. I turned to confront him, but he moved past me and headed to the back of the store, then down a hall that looked private.

I turned away from his retreating figure to the sounds of moaning on the other side of the wall. There was a small classroom in the corner of the storefront. The door was open.

Inside, I saw couples; men and women, women paired with women, men paired with men. In each pairing, one partner lay on the floor on a set of cushions. The other partner sat next to them. The partners who lay on the floor had beautiful woven blankets covering their midsections. Their legs lay straight out and their arms were above their heads or out in a T.

It reminded me of the Crucifixion. Though not a single person looked distressed. Everyone's eyes were closed as they all moaned deeply, gutturally, like a chant. My eye caught the sign on the door. Orgasmic Meditation, it read.

My eyes bulged out of my head. I turned back to the people spread out on the pillow-littered floor.

They were all fully clothed. No one was touching anyone else.

Was this a way to achieve an orgasm? Just through deep breathing and groaning? They sounded exactly like the women in the online porn videos. But no one was fussing with their hair, or looking around for a camera.

My eyes fell to the person leading the chant. He was older, with a white beard and a gentle smile that reminded me of the preacher at my grandparents' church. My ears turned back to the chanting which called to mind the hymns we used to sing on Sunday mornings. There had been such a feeling of community and love and devotion sitting in the pews.

With the chanting filling my ears, I felt weightless. My spirit felt lulled to enter the room, to join in on the praise song. But then the partners, who were all kneeling, reached beneath the blankets. I couldn't see anything but the movements of their hands beneath the covers. Were they touching...? They couldn't be. Could they?

"Can I help you?"

My body jerked as I turned to see a woman who looked like she'd stepped out of the 60's flower child movement. She could've easily been my mother's contemporary with her white blonde hair, deep blue eyes, and smooth skin. But this woman's look was effortless, natural. Not forced and controlled like my mother's.

"What are you looking for, my dear?" she asked. "Wait, let me guess?"

My throat seized as I watched and waited for her to make up her mind about me and my proclivities. What if she took me to the dildos on the opposite side of the store? Or over to the lesbian video collection in the corner?

"You're here for the Candida movies," she said after a brief pause. "Am I right? I pulled them aside for you."

"Thank you," I breathed in relief.

Candida Royalle was the maker of women-centered, art porn that promised authentic portrayals of love-making and sensuality.

"You should also check out her book, *How to Tell a Naked Man What to Do*. It teaches women to take control of their own sex life. It's perfect if you're having trouble getting your partner to please you."

"Oh, no. It's not for me. I mean it is, but not in that way. You see, I'm a writer."

"Ah, for research then?" She guided me to the cash register and began the process of ringing me up. "Is your new book fiction or nonfiction?"

I hesitated. But this woman was not my mother. She seemed interested in what I was doing for a living. Definitely not my mother.

"Fiction," I said. "I've been writing sweet romance novels, but my publisher wants me to add steam and open doors to the love scenes."

The woman nodded sagely as she handed back my credit card. "Writing sex is not as easy as insert tab A into slot B. It's about emotion and feeling and communication."

Emotion and feeling, I understood. It was the tabs into slots I was utterly clueless about. Not utterly. I knew what went where. I just didn't know how to describe them with the emotion and feeling of the act. Everything I'd seen had been faked. But these videos I was purchasing were supposed to be the real deal, full of emotion and feeling. The closest thing to voyeurism without being in physical attendance.

She handed the package to me and leaned over the counter as though our business dealing was not yet over. "You know, I was just having this conversation with my -Christopher, come here for a second."

I turned and saw the blond speedster carrying a box of what looked like large pacifiers. He got closer, his eyes lighting on me. When he came up beside me, I saw the label on the box. It read; Anal Plugs.

CHAPTER FOUR

"CHRISTOPHER," said the older woman. "This is... I'm sorry, dear. I didn't get your name?"

I hadn't left my name when I'd called in earlier. I'd just said I'd be by to pick up the items. Staring into Christopher's fathomless, blue eyes again, I lost my sense. Something inside told me to tell him everything. And so I did.

"Mary Katherine. Mary Katherine Wallace."

"That's a lovely name. I'm Holly and this is Christopher. Christopher, Ms. Wallace here is an author. She's doing research for her novel."

I expected the guy to blanch at the idea of talking about books. Instead, his blue eyes lit up. I had to brace myself by leaning into the counter from the impact. I was an absolute sucker for handsome men. It didn't cause me much trouble. I so rarely spoke to drop dead gorgeous model types.

Christopher gave me his full attention. And then he spoke to me. "Anything I would know?" he asked.

I wrestled to untie my tongue. "I doubt it. Unless you read romance novels?"

"Read them? I inhaled Harlequins as a teenaged boy. The chance to get inside a girl's head? Why would I pass up that opportunity?"

I couldn't tell if he was joking or not? His tone was serious, but mischief clouded those blue of his eyes. Then his face sobered. The mischief fled his gaze and an intelligent front moved in.

"But I have complaints," he said. "A lot of those books set women up for unrealistic expectations."

He sat the box of anal plugs on the counter. Then he motioned me towards a table with chairs. He preceded me and pulled out a chair, looking up at me expectantly.

I was too shocked to do anything but follow.

"Take for example the grand gesture," he continued once we both were seated. "It's the guy that's always in the wrong and has to make an apology speech. But both the guy and the girl have a part in the problem, or the misunderstanding. Then there's the happily-ever-after. The book ends just when everything's getting started, when we all know for a fact that every couple has their ups and downs, and many relationships don't last the first year. My parents have been together for thirty years. They fuss and they fight, but my dad says he wakes up every morning and reaches for my mother, even when he's mad at her."

My toes curled up into the clouds. My ovaries had heart palpitations. On the other side of the wall, I heard the Orgasmic Meditation group. Their chants were no longer in synch. They were also no longer in harmony. Some cries rang higher, others lower.

"But my biggest gripe," Christopher continued his sermon over the chorus of guttural praises in the next room, "is the simultaneous orgasm. Do you know how hard that is to achieve? And not all women are multi-orgasmic. But they expect the guy to do all the work, and all she has to do is lay there. That's what romance novels teach women."

The bell ringing over the entry door broke up the chanting and his speech. Two women entered the shop.

They were both tall with legs for days. The first was pancake thin in a low-cut blouse and hip-hugging skirt. The second was shaped like a soda bottle with a slim torso and then a flaring backside that couldn't be real. But as I looked closer at their faces, I realized that they had to be twins.

"Hi, Ms. Holly," they said in unison.

"Hello, girls," said Holly with a welcoming smile. "Your order came in this morning. I'll grab it for you." She disappeared down the private hall.

"Hey, Crow," purred Soda Bottle. "I hear your crew is having a party tonight."

"We're coming over," said Pancake. "You wanna come to our place for some pre-party fun?"

"Thanks ladies, but no. I'm talking to my new friend, MK."

Pancake and Soda Bottle glanced at me. Holly came out of the back with a package in her hands and motioned the girls over to the cash register. They went without a huff. By the time I turned back around, Christopher, or was it Crow, had his eyes back on me.

"So, tell me about your story, MK."

I looked between the twins and him. They looked like the type of women who knew how to tell a naked man what to do. I'd never even seen a naked man in real life. This, sitting across a table from Christopher, was the closest I'd been to a man in months. "You should probably go with them."

"I'll hook up with them later," he said.

"You could probably get lucky with them. You should know that's not going to happen with me."

The mischief returned to his blue eyes. "I wasn't aware that I'd offered sex. I thought we were having a conversation."

The tips of my ears burned bright red. Of course he wasn't interested in me. Not when he had twin models throwing themselves at him. "I'm sorry. I realize I'm not your type-"

"No," he chuckled. "You're exactly my type, MK."

I liked my name. I thought it made me unique having two first names. Being called two letters by this man with an angelic face and the devil in his eyes, made me feel like a different version of myself. Someone hip and cool.

I shook myself out of it. Inside, I was the same old Mary Katherine. "I'm a virgin."

That should do it. When I laid that bit of knowledge on the men I dated that got them leaning back in their chairs and raising their hand for the check. Christopher leaned back in his chair, but his hand didn't rise to call forth the end of our time together. The look on his face began as a grimace, but it kept spreading wider and wider, like the Cheshire cat.

"Oh, MK." He shook his head as he rubbed his

thumb across his grinning lips. "I've got a thing for virgins."

He looked at me with interest. He specifically looked at my chest with interest, like he was debating the best way to get me out of my sundress.

I crossed my arms over my chest. "I'm waiting until marriage."

He cocked his head, curious but undaunted. "For religious reasons?"

I was shocked that we were still having this conversation. Most guys would have run for the hills by this time. "Are you trying to figure out the rules of some game?"

He leaned back in his chair, smile still in place. "You're the one who keeps putting your cherry on a platter. I was simply enjoying your company."

"You're leering at my breasts," I said.

He shrugged, completely unapologetic. "I've got a thing for breasts. And your body is smoking hot. It's not illegal to look."

He was joking. He had to be joking. I was twenty pounds overweight, thirty if you asked my mother. Christopher was a golden god. He could go after the sure things, like Pancake and Soda Bottle who were waving goodbye as they left the shop. So why was he staying with me?

His eyes were fastened on mine. Intelligence pushing aside the mischief once more. "How are you going to write sex scenes with no sexual experience?"

The moan of a woman from the other room punctuated his question. I bit the inside of my cheek.

I looked up at Christopher, who continued to rub his thumb against his lip as he considered me. The motion was hypnotic. My tongue snuck out and licked at my lips. "Are you going to offer me some experience?"

His eyes zeroed in on my tongue. He pinched the spot on his lip that mirrored where my tongue had just landed on my bottom lip. I shut my eyes as I realized he was right. I had just offered up my cherry on a platter to him again.

"I'm sorry," I said. "I don't know why I said that?"

"I'm not after your panties, MK. You're not my type."

My head jerked back giving me whiplash.

"Physically, yes. But mentally, no. You're a Mrs. Forever. I'm a Mr. Right Now."

"Meaning," I said, "you're not the settling down

and marrying kind? Or if you did, you would cheat on your wife."

"I've never cheated anyone in my life." Christopher frowned, looking like a petulant child and reminding me of my sister's boys. "I'll fuck those two girls tonight. They'll both know I fucked the other one. Hell, I'll probably fuck them both at the same time. Might fuck another girl after that. I don't lie to girls to get what I want. I tell them the truth, and if it's not something they want, I move along. I've never forced anyone to do anything... unless they asked me to."

Again, I saw the flash of the devil hidden behind that angelic face.

"Plus," he continued with that Cheshire grin, "I have a short attention span. I couldn't keep all the lies straight in my head."

Why was I still sitting and listening to this guy? And why was I still hearing his voice reining me in from up high on Cloud Nine? He was everything I didn't want in a life partner. Mainly, because he had no intentions of being anyone's life partner. He worked in a sex shop. He drove a fast car and broke the speed limit. He admitted that he slept with multiple women at the same time.

"Most would say I'm more honest than they'd

care to hear," Christopher said. "I have no intentions of getting married. That's a condition of having sex with you, right?"

I couldn't respond. My ears were still replaying him talking about having sex with me.

"Therefore, I have no intentions of taking your virginity because that's not a responsibility I'm willing to commit to."

He was right. That was more honesty than I cared to hear. "So, why are you still here?"

"I never met a romance writer before," he grinned, letting go of his serious side. "I'm interested. My mother calls me insatiably curious. So tell me, how do you keep your readers interested with no sex?"

He'd picked up the conversation about my work again, as though we hadn't been discussing both of our vastly different sex lives. My head was spinning from all the directions my attention was being pulled toward.

There was the crescendoing sounds coming from behind the wall. There was the sound of the bell dinging letting customers in. The sound of Holly's cheery voice as she greeted them. And then there was Christopher, sitting before me with an attentiveness I hadn't had since my grandparents passed away a few years ago.

"Relationships aren't all about sex," I said.

He frowned in disbelief.

"They're not," I insisted. "They're about connection and emotion over time. Love happens emotionally, spiritually, before the physical. Victorian and Regency romances were hundreds of pages long with only a kiss on the last page. Yet, it was clear the hero and heroine were in love by the middle. You really know it's true before all the sex clouds your brain."

Christopher grinned. "How would you know that sex clouds the brain?"

"Doesn't it?"

He didn't answer, but I got the distinct impression, even with the mischief in his grin, that his brain never got clouded.

"People get stupid," I said. "Two women are willing to sleep with you, one after the other, or at the same time."

"And you think that makes them stupid? Chrissy is an engineer and Fiona created her own startup. They're two intelligent women who have a sex positive view of their bodies. Satisfaction is a powerful emotion, a relaxing emotion that provides clarity -at least for me."

The crescendoes in the other room were coming fewer and further between, like the last few seconds of a bag of popcorn turning in the microwave.

"If you believe so strongly in what you're doing with the sweet romance," he said, "why change it?"

"Sex sells. And if I want to keep my publishing contract, I have to write about it."

He leaned forward. "But you don't want to?"

I shook my head.

"That sounds like an abuse of power to me."

I couldn't disagree. It was akin to a boyfriend demanding his girlfriend have sex with him or he'd break up with her. I didn't want to break up with my career. I loved what I did. I loved weaving stories of romance, of having two people from opposite spectrums come together, and making their lives together work.

"One thing I do know is that the experience of an orgasm is something you can't plagiarize," he said. "Guys might not be able to tell when a woman is faking it, but another woman can."

He was right about that. I'd watched enough opening scenes of porn to be the judge.

"If you need a hand with writing those parts," he

leaned further forward, bracing his elbows on the table, "let me know. I'll help you."

I pulled back slighty. My hand rose off the table like I was in grade school. "I have to ask again, but I mean it this time. Are you trying to get into my panties?"

He laughed out loud. "I don't have to get into your panties to show you what an orgasm feels like. Give me your hand."

CHAPTER FIVE

MY FINGERS TWITCHED like a nerve had been pinched and was trying to break free. My pinky finger stuck out straight as though struck by lightning. My thumb curled into my palm. The three fingers in the middle flexed forward as though reaching out for Christopher, who watched my twitchy fingers with amusement.

I balled all my fingers into a fist. "What are you going to do?"

His blue eyes locked onto mine and held. If carnal was a color, it would be found in Christopher's eyes. He grinned, reminding me of a puppy dog. "Trust me."

His hand lay open on the table across from mine. Not moving close. Not retreating away.

One by one my fingers unfurled. I watched them in puzzlement, trying to work out why. The scary thing was that I did; I trusted him. There was something about Christopher that told me I could.

Was it those clear blue eyes that hid nothing and let me see his every intention? Was it that mischievous grin that urged me to come out and play? Was it the fact that I had his undivided attention and had somehow managed to hold his interest?

My grandfather always told me that people tell you who they are when you first meet them. The problem was that listeners often choose to ignore the truth. Christopher told me exactly who he was. He'd said it to my face. The question was would I listen?

I placed my hand in his. His was warm. A slight hum of energy zinged between us. He ran his thumb along the sides of my thumb and then my pinky finger. The tremors stopped. A sense of calm flooded through me.

He placed his other hand below mine and continued to graze my skin lightly. "What do you feel?"

Like I was lying in a cradle of warmth. "Safe."

My fingers flexed. I had not meant to say that. But it was what I felt. I'd never had anyone hold my hand as an adult.

I wrote about men holding women's hands. I'd never experienced it in real life. The words I'd written didn't do this simple gesture justice. I couldn't tell him that. So, I did what any writer worth her ink would do. I reached into my writer's toolbox for a metaphor.

"I mean," I tried again, "your fingers are cradling mine. So, it reminded me of the hammock in my grandparents' backyard. I'd lie there for hours reading and no one bothered me. My grandma would bring me honey tea and cheese sandwiches. My grandpa would kiss my forehead as he worked in his vegetable garden. Your fingers are warm and they reminded me of the feeling of the sun on my skin. The hammock was under a tree so when I swung I'd go in and out of the light. With your touch, the pads of your fingers are the warmth, and in between are the clouds. I felt safe in that hammock."

I stopped, realizing I'd dug myself into an even deeper hole with my purple prose. I looked up into Christopher's clear, blue eyes. I couldn't read his expression.

He looked... enraptured? That couldn't be right. It was more flowery nonsense spewing from my writer's tool kit. He probably thought I was some little girl lost.

"Not that I was unsafe anywhere else." I didn't want him to get the impression I came from an abusive family. Dysfunctional, sure. Abusive, no.

Christopher squeezed my palm. He grazed his fingers over my wrist. The sensation shot up my arm like an electric shock, right into my chest. A shudder went down my spine and I let out a trembling sound.

His eyes widened in surprise. Or was that male gloating? He'd gotten me to spew nonsense and now he'd gotten a physical reaction from me. He probably saw a clear pathway to my panties.

I tried to yank my hand away, but his long fingers closed around my wrist. They were light enough to let me know that I could get away. They were firm enough to let me know he wanted me to stay.

"Wait," he said softly. "Tell me what you felt just then?"

His eyes were earnest as they looked into mine. There was no gloating. Only curiosity. Could that be right?

"I like the way you describe things, MK." He

grazed the pulse point over my wrist. "It never occurred to me that such a light touch could be so sexy. Tell me? How would you describe that in a book?"

My head spun as my pulse raced. Here was a guy asking me for my favorite thing. He wanted me to tell him a story. There was no way I could resist. I stopped struggling and let him have my hand.

I closed my eyes and pictured the hero in my book. Unsurprisingly, the hero had blond hair and blue eyes. "When his fingers slid down her wrists, her blood wanted to reverse course and follow. His touch stopped my heart and changed the course of my life."

The room fell silent. The chorus of meditative orgasms stopped. No new customers dinged into the door. Holly's cheery chatter muted as well.

I opened my eyes. There was a small smile of satisfaction on Christopher's face. "I meant to say *her* eyes, not *my* eyes."

He tilted his head in acknowledgment, but I didn't think he believed me.

"I stand corrected," he said. "That totally turned me on. And you're not even naked. You're very good."

A tremor went up my palm which still lay in his

hand. His hold tightened slightly, just a firm caress. Everything in me slowed. The tremors, my pulse, my heartbeat, my sense of self-preservation. My doubts of who he'd told me he was.

I thrilled at his praise, feeling for the first time that I could do this. I could throw the door wide open and write this steamy book.

"What are you going to do about penetration?" he asked.

And just like that, everything came crashing down.

"Please don't do the crashing waves or any water references," he said. "I don't know any guy who would want his moves compared to a woman drowning."

"I don't know? I haven't gotten that far."

He grinned at the double meaning of my words. I hadn't gotten that far in my intimate life nor in the book's plot.

"You don't need to be penetrated to have an orgasm." His words were thoughtful. He gazed off into the distance, still holding and caressing my wrist and fingers.

A tingling sensation made its way up my arm. My breathing shallowed. I should probably take my hand back. Instead, I pressed my thighs together.

"You could just describe the sensations you feel from masturbating."

He didn't look at me as he said it. But in the silence that ensued he turned those blue lasers back on me. It took him only a second to review the x-ray of my red face and make a diagnosis. I knew it was clearly written on my face that I'd never touched myself in that way.

"I can help you with that," he prescribed. "If you'd like."

"You want to help me masturbate?" I pulled my hand away then.

There it was. He'd been trying to get inside my panties the whole time. I should've known better. I should've listened. I was nothing but a conquest to a guy like this.

"You don't have to get naked," he said, eyes smiling like he'd seen my every thought. "And I won't touch anything you don't want me to. I can get you close to coming just touching erogenous zones that don't touch where your bathing suit does."

I heard this man loud and clear. I believed him. He looked at me with those fathomless eyes, hiding nothing. My fingers, which had balled into another fist, unfurled once more.

But there was no way I was doing this. I couldn't

possibly do this. Was I actually considering doing this?

The sound of a whistle cracked the air, muting the ringing of the bell over the shop's open door. A dark figure stood in the door. The same man who had raced down the street with Christopher walked in.

Without his sunglasses on, his hazel eyes did a slow scan of my body, taking his time at the slow curve of my ample bosom on down to my wide hips which took up the whole plastic seat of the chair. He sucked in his bottom lip as his journey reached my thick thighs, which were pressed together under the table.

I wanted to say something, but I couldn't. I thought of any number of sassy quips, but my throat went dry as his eyes heated my limbs. Those blazing eyes stayed on mc as he spoke to Christopher.

"Yo, Crow? You ready?"

Crow seemed an odd nickname for Christopher? Why not Chris? Or the more popular Topher?

"No, I'll catch you later," Christopher said, leaning back in his chair. His eyes were also on my breasts. "I'm still working here."

The other man's lip curled into a smile that

would make the devil shiver. "She coming to the party tonight?"

Christopher's eyes found mine. The edges crinkled as he gave me all of his focus. "No, she's not like that."

There was disappointment in his voice. There was also certainty. It shouldn't have mattered. I didn't want to go to this party where he was planning to have sex with two or three women.

But part of him wanted me there. That thought thrilled me.

"She looks sweet," said his friend who still hung in the doorway.

"I'll catch you later, Eagle." Christopher tossed over his shoulder.

Eagle turn to head out of the door. "Selfish son-of-a-bitch," he murmured. The ringing bell punctuated his exit.

"Friend of yours?" I asked.

Christopher shrugged. "Just one of my brothers."

I didn't remark that they were of different races.

"How many brothers do you have?" As the words left my lips, I realized that I didn't know this guy. But a moment ago I had been seriously considering letting him touch me where my bathing suit touched me. A moment after that, I'd been contemplating an invitation to a party where he'd be having sex with other girls.

This had been a fun stop in dreamland, but it was time to get back to the real world where heroes sought out their fated mates, fell in love at first sight, and made grand overtures in their apologies for a big misunderstanding.

I gathered my things. "I should go."

"But we weren't finished."

I stopped and looked at him. He was pouting again, complete with the puppy dog eyes. But I saw it. There was the devilish curl to his lip that told me he wanted to make mischief.

"Why didn't you invite me to your party?" I asked.

It wasn't what I had planned to say, but those were the words that wanted to come out. That often happened when I was writing. I'd plot the story, but sometimes the characters hijacked it and took me where they needed to go instead of where I thought was best.

Christopher tilted his head back and peered up at me. "You mean, the party where I'm going to fuck those two girls? It's not your scene, MK. You're not the type of girl to be fucked with. You're a princess looking for a fairytale. I'm not a prince. Neither is Eagle or any of my brothers."

Again, was that disappointment I heard in his voice? Or was it my imagination?

Normally, at this point in my books the hero tells the heroine all the reasons they can't be together. But over the course of the story, they both grow and change. Is that what was happening now? Was Christopher listing all the ways that he would change? As the pages turned, would we find our way to a happily-ever-after?

"But I do want to give you an orgasm," he said.

I heard the pages crumbling in my head and falling onto the floor with a loud thunk.

"I want to hear what you have to say about it. I like listening to you describe things."

His eyes sparkled, an angel asking for my soul, and I swear to God, that was the moment I lost my heart to the man I knew I would spend the rest of my life with.

But of course, it's not that simple. There's a few mountains these two need to climb first.

And not just on her chest!

Start Crow and MK's story now!
Read Dangerous Curves Ahead, Book 3 in the Watchers Crew series.

DANGEROUS CURVES *Ahead* **is the third book in the Watchers Crew series; a scorching hot, urban erotic romance series that explores themes of domination, menage, and open relationships.**

If you like your heroes alpha and multiple, then you'll love the men of the Watchers Crew.

Buy *Dangerous Curves Ahead* today and explore a world where there's always a happy ending, but it's shared.

Lover of fairytales, folklore, and mythology, Ines Johnson spends her days reimagining the stories of old in a modern world. She writes books where damsels cause the distress, princesses wield swords, and moms save the world.

You can sign up for her mailing list and receive alerts and free reads at http://bit.ly/InesReaders.

The Watchers Crew

Test Drive

Cruise Control

Dangerous Curves Ahead

Slippery When Wet

Smart Baztard

a free story in the world of the Watchers Crew available exclusively to

Ines Johnson's Readers Group.